TREGARTHUR'S SERIES

BOOK 4

TREGARTHUR'S CRYSTAL

 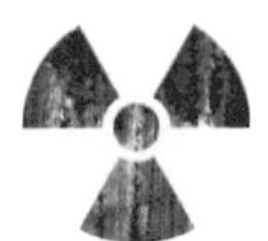   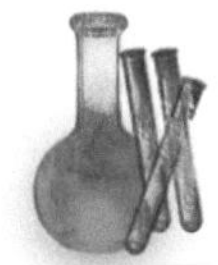

Alex Mellanby

Cillian Press

First published in Great Britain in 2017
by Cillian Press Limited. 83 Ducie Street, Manchester M1 2JQ
www.cillianpress.co.uk

British Library Cataloguing in Publication Data.
A catalogue record for this book is available from the British Library.

Paperback ISBN: 978-1-909776-20-3
eBook ISBN: 978-1-909776-21-0

Cover Photography: 'Eiffel Tower 2'

'Lost Places' by Michael Gaida.

Published by
Cillian Press – Manchester - 2017
www.cillianpress.co.uk

This book is dedicated, as before, to Pat Read and all the walkers who have and will take up the challenge of the Ten Tors. I hope the weather on Dartmoor is never this bad.

Thanks to Paul Smith, the archivist for Thomas Cook who provided help with foreign travel in the 1900s. Also thanks for the inspiration from the wonderful photographs of Paris by Eugène Atget (1857-1927). His 'Marchand d'abat-jour' could be no one other than a spy.

Cillian Press have, as always, been fantastic and patiently waited for this story to appear. Carolyn's perpetual re-reading and helpful critique has so helped me to bring this story alive.

Contents

CONTENTS

PROLOGUE

I am Alvin Carter, probably sixteen, but that might be sixteen thousand or more because I've seen cavemen, the Black Death and convicts transported to Australia.

The stones of the moor guard a way through time and Miss Alice Tregarthur with her stolen crystal controlled that gateway. Her plan is my death.

This time Jenna and I, we will stop her, we must stop her.

-1-

The Search Begins

Why Jenna, why? Why am I still up here on this damp muddy hill? Seconds earlier we were heading home. Then you took me by the arm. I know where we are; but I have no idea about the when.

'Why is it always raining?' I moaned.

'It's only drizzle.' Jenna smiled at me.

'It's always drizzle.' I smiled back. 'That's unless it's a storm, a gale, or an earthquake.'

We sheltered under the overhang of nearby rocks. The sky cleared. I was wrong. Sometimes the moor can be bright and beautiful. Behind us were the Hanging Stones. Surely this strange balanced formation could never be just one piece of stone? Wisps of hazy smoke still blew in the air, smoke that signalled a way through time; smoke that would soon be gone.

'You'll tell me why?' I spoke my thoughts to Jenna.

Perhaps she was about to reply, or at least to nod. But a gunshot echoed against the rocks below and we scrabbled forward to look, staying close to the ground. We heard shouts. Further down the hill there were three people and a horse. We knew those three, not the horse. All three wanted me dead.

The older woman had the gun. Her hair blew like straw in the wind, her cloak billowed around her. Miss Alice Tregarthur, once our crazy teacher, was reloading. The other two ran in our direction, screaming and shouting and stumbling over rough ground. The murderous Zach, previously just a playground bully, fell to the ground. Demelza, once the school queen bitch, dropped beside him – still screaming. Miss Tregarthur, failing to reload her ancient pistol another time, roared a curse before jumping on the horse and riding away at speed.

Jenna jumped up. 'Come on,' she shouted, setting off down the hill towards the fallen pair.

'Help him,' Demelza pleaded, leaning over Zach, who groaned as blood seeped through his shirt. Her words were for Jenna. I was the last person to ask for help.

'Leave him,' I said, cross that only one of them had been shot.

Jenna turned on me, her face inches from mine. No words, just her hard stare as she waited for me to climb down, as she knew I would. And I did. No point in my arguing with Jenna. She meant too much to me. I never understood how she had become a caring person. Her life story had made her such a hard girl at school and although that hardness often broke through, it didn't at that moment.

A few minutes later I was carrying Zach's bleeding body back up to the Hanging Stones. We lowered him on the ground. Only the faintest haze of smoke remained until Jenna walked towards the stones and the mist grew thicker. Was this really a sign that the time tunnel would open again?

The smoke was enough for Demelza, who ran forward, darting under the rock, trying to escape. I didn't really care if I never saw her again and I stayed where I was. Zach was coming round, still groaning. I guess he saw the mist and he started crawling towards it. The grass stained red underneath him.

'Jen,' I shouted, watching Zach but doing nothing. I was losing them all in the mist. 'Come back. Do I let him go?'

Jenna returned, with Demelza in a headlock. Despite Demelza squirming, wrestling and trying to bite and scream, Jenna had a firm hold. Jenna's hardness had returned and she squeezed tighter.

I could still see the smoky mist. Shouldn't we all try to leave? Jenna shook her head, reading my thoughts again. She had led me here and whatever her reasons, I was going to stay with her.

Zach disappeared. 'He's gone,' Jenna said. I could see that he had disappeared and so had the mist. Jenna seemed certain the tunnel had taken him. I didn't understand how she knew that. Something else had happened. Had I heard Jenna actually talking to the rocks?

Jenna dropped Demelza on the grass. 'What happened?' she asked.

'Miss Tregarthur just shot him,' Demelza snapped. 'And why didn't you let us all go? We could have got away, gone home.'

That was the same question I wanted to ask.

Jenna wasn't going to explain yet. 'Why did she shoot him?'

Demelza huffed and turned away.

'I'll ask you one more time. If you don't start talking, then it's time for pain.' Jenna, the very hard girl, said. 'So, why did she shoot him?'

In the silence Jenna said to me, 'Alvin, could you get a few pieces of wood together and light a fire?'

I turned away rather than laugh as Jenna hid her smile.

'You wouldn't?' Demelza looked at us, her face screwed up as though we'd already started.

'I thought we'd burn her to death,' Jenna said, with her hand hiding her mouth. 'After she talks.'

That might seem a little harsh and I didn't really believe Jenna would do it, but only just a *little* harsh. If I'd been alone … well. Demelza and Zach had sentenced us to burn to death in the village of the Black Death. Demelza needed to take the threat seriously.

'I'll get the wood.' I could see a few scrubby trees a few yards away.

'Wait,' Demelza blurted as I walked away. 'We came out of the tunnel, went down the hill and she just fired her gun at him.'

'Why?' I asked, gathering a few sticks, thinking I'd need a lot more. 'Why would she shoot him? You've done all the terrible things she wanted you to do. Something else must have happened.'

Demelza hiccupped a sob and tried to scrabble away. Jenna resumed the headlock while I made a pile of the twigs.

'Zach snatched the crystal from her. We just wanted to go home.' Demelza spoke with difficulty being half strangled. 'She shot at him, missed but he dropped it and we ran off. She still got him with the next shot.'

'It's always the crystal.' Jenna let go of Demelza and lent forward with her head in her hands. 'Zach had it and we should have helped him to keep it.'

Was that right? Why would we let it get into Zach's hands, or Demelza's? The shimmering crystal was the way Miss Tregarthur controlled the time tunnel, forcing it to obey her orders. But it was done by torture. No one could forget the terrible scream of agony that came from the Hanging Stones each time she crashed her iron bar down on the crystal. That was how she made time work for her.

'It has to get back to the tunnel,' Jenna turned to me. 'The crystal is part of it, something alive within the rock, without it there is only pain, I felt that awful pain. We must get it back. Alvin, that's why I wanted you to come with me. We have to do this.'

'And if we do get it back?' I said.

'The tunnel will take us home. It took Zach with his injury; it will take us.' There was something missing in Jenna's words.

'And if we don't get it back?' I said, adding the missing part.

'The crystal won't work,' Demelza butted in. 'It's running out.'

We said nothing and waited.

Demelza went on: 'The crystal was starting to fade, the light inside it is going out. It's not going to work much longer, that's why Zach grabbed it.'

Her voice became more hopeless. 'We're never going to get anywhere. If her crystal thing is finished, we're stuck here forever.' Demelza could see the effect of her words. 'You can do what you like to me but it won't make any difference.'

'Did she try to call the tunnel again?' Jenna asked.

'She tried and tried, hitting that thing before you arrived. I was expecting the screaming noise to start, but nothing happened. I tell you we're stuck; not going anywhere. She said there was no way it was ever going to work again.'

'Why didn't she shoot you?' I asked, thinking it would have been a good idea.

'She just ran off saying something about curry, or that's what I heard.'

'Curry?' Jenna and I shouted together.

We were still sitting around the Hanging Stones and it wasn't getting any warmer. We would have to leave, to get off the moor.

'Jen,' I said. 'It's not always … not always about the crystal, is it? This time it took Zach. You didn't have the crystal.'

'It does what it wants,' Jenna said. 'Sometimes it will even do what you want.'

'It won't do that now, will it?' Demelza said, getting angry. 'Will it Jenna? Tell us why it won't take us anywhere now.'

Jenna just stared out into the moor.

'It won't do anything until we bring back the crystal,' Demelza was on her feet shouting. 'That's it, isn't it? That's what you've agreed. I heard you. You've agreed that with this tunnel thing.' I think Demelza added words under her breath like stupid and worse.

Jenna was up and ready for a fight. But her fists dropped and I could see tears in her eyes. 'I had no choice. Whatever has happened to the crystal we must still get it back.'

Something in the absolute pain of the tunnel had worked into Jenna's mind. I could see Demelza thinking this through – no crystal, no going home. She would have to stay with us, at least until we found Miss Tregarthur.

'Well, if that's what we have to do, we'd better get on with it, come on.' I led the way down the hill and the other two followed. If this was what Jenna had agreed, then I would do it with her.

We were going after Miss Tregarthur. It hadn't been difficult to see which way she went; it was a direction we had taken before in a different time.

After we had been walking for a while Demelza stopped. 'Why didn't you let me go with Zach? You don't need me; you could have let me go.'

'Oh, but we do need you,' Jenna pushed her onwards. 'We need you to tell us everything you know. And if you don't, then striking you with an iron bar will be much too gentle for you.'

'But I've told you everything,' Demelza stumbled.

'No you haven't. You really haven't. Keep walking.' Jenna pushed her again.

Hours later we stumbled into the village on the edge of the moor.

'Rats?' I said. This was a place we knew, where so many had died of the plague, in the time of the Black Death.

'It's not the same time.' Jenna pointed to an inn with a sign above it, promising ale and beds for the night. 'It's not the same. Different houses.'

There were fewer old wooden buildings, fewer buildings altogether. There were no wires, no electric lights to light the early evening. We were not in our own time.

'It's nearer though?' Jenna said, looking around.

'Nearer to what?' I was confused.

Jenna stood in front of me. 'Not so far back in time. I think we're getting nearer to our own time. We never go back further than we have been already.'

'That's because she's worn it out.' Demelza did have more to say: 'The tunnel thing is getting weaker along with the crystal. Miss Tregarthur had wanted to return to the time of the cavemen but it didn't work, no matter how many times Miss Tregarthur hit it.'

'Anything more you've forgotten to tell us?' Jenna turned on her.

'No, nothing,' Demelza squirmed away getting closer to me. I felt she did that on purpose. She hadn't told us everything, but I was tired and hungry and didn't feel like another struggle. I went towards the inn.

'No money,' Jenna said, as we stood outside. 'Just the two leftover coins we had from our time before.' She repeated, 'No other money.'

Jenna was making it pretty clear that I needed to keep quiet about the gold belt I had wound around my arm, a reward for saving the King of England back in the time of the Black Death. The belt needed to stay hidden, it was just too valuable. We were lucky to have it at all, rescued from one of Miss Tregarthur's relatives.

We went in through the inn's old wooden door, which creaked loudly as we entered. The bar was just a room, full of smoke. In one corner, I could just make out three old men who stopped talking and stared at us when we walked in. A grubby looking woman in a worn apron and ragged clothes sat in front of the smouldering fire peeling a few potatoes. She muttered something about more people.

'What do you want?' She was the landlady and not too pleased about it.

It turned out that the two coins were worth enough for a night at the inn. Did that mean they were still in use, that we hadn't moved very far forward in time? I didn't think it meant anything, the coins were probably silver and that was valuable.

The inn was a poor place. The landlady called for 'Tom' who showed us up to a room.

She said the room came with food in the bar – bread and mouldy potatoes. I worried about going into the bar – how would we answer questions? What would Demelza say and would she try to run off?

The three men still sat in the dark smoky room, big enough to take more people. It looked like they could have been there for some time, days possibly, and were drinking their way through anything the inn had left. One of the men slipped off his seat when we entered the bar and started snoring. When he did wake up he started going on about machinery.

'The devil's business,' he slurred. 'Who are you?' he pointed at me.

I was wondering what to say but there was no need. He turned to the others, and they went back to arguing about machines and why everyone had left the village. Often repeating that it was the 'devil's business'. Actually nearly all their conversation was repeating things and calling for more drink.

'Moving for money,' the landlady muttered. 'That's where he's gone.'

'Her husband,' cackled one of old men. 'Best rid of him, Bettie.'

She'd been abandoned with her son, Tom. This place wasn't going to make a life for them. The men drinking weren't paying, just taking advantage in the absence of the landlord. Once again this village was losing the young men, just like in the time of the Black Death.

We did get a few more questions.

'From Poland,' I used the cover story we'd used once before and we tried to talk in the chopped speech one of us had used last time.

'Foreign, eh?'

That seemed to satisfy the men, being foreign and not knowing anything about machines meant we weren't interesting. Whenever Demelza looked like saying anything, Jenna poked her under the table; Jenna's pokes are very hard.

Later we creaked up the stairs to our room, one room. I let the girls have the bed. Well that's not actually true. I'd suggested we all shared, with Demelza in the middle in case she changed her mind and did run off.

But Jenna didn't like the look on Demelza's face when she said, with a coy smile: 'Share the bed with Alvin, fine by me.' Nor probably the look on my face either. I got the floor.

'Do we really need to keep her with us?' I asked when we were woken in the night by creaks, groans and scuttling – I didn't think all the rats had left. 'She's no use and doesn't seem to know anything.'

We might have an idea how Miss Tregarthur controlled things or couldn't control things now. I didn't see why we needed to drag Demelza around with us and the floor wasn't comfortable.

'Why?' I asked, not caring whether Demelza heard my question. 'Why do we need her?'

'Maybe in case we need someone else to get shot,' Jen replied and turned over with nothing more to say. Demelza gave another squeal, although I think she actually blew me a kiss. I felt more confusion, sensed more danger.

The morning brought rain and a bowl of gruel which reminded

me of stews Jenna had cooked. We sat at a table and tried to plan.

'Apart from getting the crystal, we need to find out what Miss Tregarthur's up to because I'm sure it needs to be stopped,' Jenna said.

'We've no idea where she's gone. Maybe we should just go back to the Hanging Stones?' Demelza joined in.

'What makes you think we're going to do anything you say?' Jenna said. 'Just keep your mouth shut. Nothing happens without the crystal.'

I felt Demelza could be right. We had no idea where Miss Tregarthur had gone. She hadn't stayed in this inn. She could have gone anywhere. I really wasn't going to suggest that Demelza was right. We should never have brought her along. She kept giving me little smiles and I know Jenna saw her doing it.

'Alvin, go and ask the landlady if she saw Miss Tregarthur,' Jenna ordered.

'Me?' I couldn't see why she thought I'd be any use at getting information from the landlady. She had been so miserable.

'Seems like all the women fall for you,' Jenna snapped.

I ran for it, searching out the landlady in the kitchen. I wouldn't have eaten anything if I'd seen the state of the kitchen first.

'What you want now?' The landlady scowled. She looked even worse than last night. I think she may have been working her own way through the booze. 'You'll get no more food. Didn't pay me enough.'

She turned and looked me over. 'You don't fancy staying on here?' She tried a smile which was a lot scarier than her scowl. 'Suppose not,' she said, seeing my face. 'Don't suppose anyone would fancy staying here.' She wiped her eyes. 'Not with me, anyway.'

I had no idea what to do. She looked like someone's gran and perhaps that made me get nearer and give her a hug. I got hugged back and didn't think I'd ever escape until I heard a loud cough behind me.

'How are you doing Alvin?' Jenna snapped again and I jumped away. 'Bettie' might look like someone's gran but she was probably a lot younger. Even so, surely Jen wasn't getting angry because … well because.

'I was just asking her …' I started.

'Oh yeah?'

'You didn't see someone else yesterday?' I turned to the landlady who had slumped down in her chair and must have picked up Jenna's mood.

'Like who?'

'Like some weird woman,' Jenna stepped between us. 'Weird woman with loads of wild hair, it blows about.' Jen waved her hands above her head.

'Oh her,' the landlady picked up her bowl of half peeled potatoes. She held it as though it might protect her. 'Nasty woman. She was on our old horse, said she found him on the moor, didn't believe her even though he had run off. Bought him though.' The landlady slapped the pocket in her apron to the sound of jingling coins.

'Did she say anything else, anything strange?' I asked.

'Odd you should say that,' the landlady gave me a puzzled look. 'She didn't want to stay but she asked me what year it was. I told her and she almost went berserk, screaming at me that I couldn't be right. She must be crazy, I almost thought of getting those drunks to help, but she ran off. A few minutes later though she was back and wanted to know about Masterson.'

'Masterson?' Jenna and I said together.

'Who's he?' Jen added.

'Rich bloke. Has a big house down in the village?' The landlady waved her arm in the direction of the track that led down the hill from the inn. 'Ask anyone if you want to find him.' She gave a cackle. 'That's if he wants you to find him.'

A few minutes later we were walking down the track. I didn't escape another hug. 'Just in case you change your mind about staying.' She had said while handing me back one of our coins.

'Wonder why Miss Tregarthur went crazy when she heard what year it was?' I said to Jenna after we'd gone a few steps.

'No idea. Don't suppose you know, Demelza?'

Demelza said nothing.

'Maybe the tunnel didn't do what she wanted,' Jenna said. 'Maybe the tunnel took her to the wrong time.'

Demelza huffed, slowed down and muttered about the drizzle. That got a shove from both of us, but we did walk on. I was wondering what we would do if we caught up with our crazy teacher.

Jen still had on her cross face. Demelza was winding her up, being girly and bumping into me. I kept moving away. This was a disaster and one I didn't know how to deal with. Somehow pushing her away made it worse.

'What do you think Tregarthur wants this Masterson for?' I said, for something to say.

'How does she know anyone here?' Jenna stared at me.

'She's got this book,' Demelza butted in, bumping me again.

Jen grabbed her, threw her to the ground and stood over her. 'I knew you were hiding things.'

'Alvin,' Demelza gave me a pouty look.

'And you can stop that too,' Jen gave her a kick, not too softly. 'He's not going to help you.'

'I said she's got this book – an encyclopaedia or something.' Demelza rubbed her leg. 'Carries it around under her cloak. It tells her useful stuff when she moves in time, what's happening in each year she goes to. She looked at it before … before Zach got shot.'

'She knew …' I stopped. 'She knew all about the Black Death when she sent us to that time?'

'Yes, that's why …' Demelza tried to get up.

'That's why she sent us there, we know that,' Jenna pushed her down again. 'What else does this book tell her? I suppose you know all about this Masterson?' Jenna was ready with another kick.

'Don't kick me.' Demelza curled up on the ground. 'Of course I don't know about him. She never let me see the book, just told me what it was for. That's where she found out about this curry.'

That made no sense so we set off again. Demelza walking with an exaggerated limp, which made Jenna sniff loudly. I said nothing.

Slowly I realised that this track was heading in a direction I had taken before, when Miss Tregarthur had sent us to the Black Death. We were heading towards the same town that had been almost deserted and in flames, burning the houses, the church destroyed and the Lord of the Manor's house looted and in ruins.

But that wasn't where Masterson had his big house. Bettie, the landlady, had told us his house was in one of the smaller villages. We had further to walk after we came down into the valley and had to ask for directions as we went along. We passed another inn. Locals standing outside shouted at us and it wasn't friendly. Three large dogs appeared and barked loudly. We hurried on. Made me think that the horrors of the Black Death still hung over the people who remained here.

As we walked down the road Jenna was still quiet. Eventually she turned to me, 'Alvin, how old are you?'

It was a confusing question. I was about to turn sixteen when we left on Miss Tregarthur's walk, about to leave school and about to be thrown out of the house. But we'd been away for – I really didn't know how long we'd been away. There hadn't been any birthday parties.

I gave a shrug. 'Older, I suppose.' And that was the best any of us could do as we trudged down the valley leaving the moor behind.

By the time we found Masterson's house it was starting to get dark. Dark and very quiet. We could see the shape of a large house in the distance, surrounded by fields and trees. The way to the house was blocked.

'What?' said a man standing in front of a large iron gate. The gate wasn't actually a lot taller than the man – he was huge and wearing some sort of uniform.

I wasn't going to get anywhere with him, lucky we had Jenna. She walked right up to him, right in his face. Reminded me of how she once got us into a club when we were about twelve. Jen ate bouncers.

'Masterson.' Jenna actually prodded the man in the chest.

'Not here,' the man stammered and stepped back, obviously he hadn't met a Jenna before.

'Where?' She kept it short and sharp.

'Gone to the big town … with that woman.' The man added a shiver to the stammer. He had obviously met Miss Tregarthur.

'That witch,' came a voice from just inside the gate and a woman stepped forward, she was wearing an apron and a white cap; maybe she was the cook. 'Don't know why Masterson went with her. Now you lot turn up. What do you want? 'Cos you're not going to get anything from us.'

'Which big town?' I stepped forward, worrying that this wasn't going well and wondering if they meant London.

The gate man and the woman looked at each other.

'Get the constable Ben,' the woman said firmly. 'There's something wrong with this lot, turning up in the dark, they're up to something.'

We ran.

'Ben, get after them.'

Luckily Ben might be big and scary but he was not built for running, especially since it was nearly dark and there were no street lamps here. We didn't stop and Ben didn't follow us very far.

'What now?' Demelza said, in an angry voice as though this was our fault.

Jenna pushed her into a ditch. She scrabbled out, with a bit more dirt and a nasty scowl.

Walking on we came to the inn of the not-friendly locals; not-friendly landlord either.

'What's this?' The man behind the bar looked like he knew

about trouble and his face suggested he hadn't always won his arguments. He was examining our last coin that Jenna had handed over, hoping we could get a room and some food. He even put it between his teeth and bit down on it. It might have been more valuable than we thought, but he wasn't going to let us know that.

'This is all you'll get,' he slapped a lump of bread on the bar, pocketed the coin. 'Now get out before I set the dogs on you.'

I was going to argue but Jenna pulled me away saying that we didn't want to be remembered here as well as at the house, especially if Ben did actually find a policeman. Demelza was pouting again.

An older man drinking in the corner shouted at her: 'You can stay love, come over here.' That brought a laugh from the two other men with him. Jenna pushed Demelza out of the door and into darkness. There was just a faint glimmer of light from the moon in a cloudy sky.

'What now?' Demelza said, again in her angry voice and stepping out of Jenna's way. 'That man, I could have …'

'No you couldn't,' Jenna shoved her again.

Demelza gave me a look. Part of me felt that using Demelza might have got us more than a lump of bread. It wasn't just Demelza looking at me though; Jenna's face told me that it just wasn't going to happen.

The best shelter we could find was an old broken down barn with half the roof fallen in, which became more of a problem when it rained. We weren't the only occupants. In one corner, under most of the remaining roof and lying on a pile of straw, were three people. A mother and two children. It took me straight back to the little family we'd met in the time of the plague – the family that had all died.

'Are they …?' I whispered to Jenna and meaning were they infectious.

'Hope not,' she understood immediately but went up to them and started talking.

'Sssh,' hissed the woman and pulled Jenna down on to the straw.

I heard someone walking on the road outside, the woman was terrified. The footsteps moved away and she relaxed. Jenna carried on talking in whispers.

While Jenna talked, Demelza and I tried to find more straw and a dry patch to spend the night. After a few minutes Jenna joined us.

'They've nowhere to go,' Jenna sounded hopeless. 'Thrown out of their house, no job, and her husband has taken up with someone else.'

We shared the lump of bread with them, without talking because they were frightened of any noise. When we woke, they'd gone.

'She said they were going down to Cornwall to find out if her sister is still there,' Jenna told us. 'She said it wasn't safe to stay here, they'd lock us up if they found us. That's what frightened her in the night. If they found her they would take the children away from her. We have to move.'

'Where?' I couldn't see how or why we were going anywhere.

'The place they called the big town, after Alice Tregarthur.' I could see Jenna knew more.

'How?'

'By train,' Jenna smiled.

'Train?' I said.

'Of course. What else?' Jenna said, as though I was stupid.

'They have trains?' Demelza sounded almost hopeful, as though we might be nearer to our own time, something she could deal with.

'Yep, the woman we met last night said that a few miles away we can catch a train which could take us to the big town. They call Exeter the big town.'

'Exeter?' That really confused me. 'I've been to Exeter.'

'Me too,' said both the girls together.

-2-

Train

We set off to find the train station. The night had left us hungry, damp and tired. In silence we walked along the road and after climbing another hill we could see a cloud of smoke hanging over houses in the valley. It wasn't difficult to find the railway station because that was where the smoke was coming from.

Arriving in the town we passed rows of houses, another poor place. Poor and smelly; whatever was happening in this century it wasn't sorting out the drains. Smell and smoke were everywhere.

'Steam trains, can you believe it?' I said, as I looked at the monstrous green engine belching smoke as it left the station.

'If I believe your train or not,' Jenna said, with hands on hips. 'It will still cost money, whatever sort of puffing thing it is.'

We had no money left. The last two days had left us looking worse, although I don't suppose I'd been really clean for ages – however long that was. But looking wild and rough actually helped us, we looked in need of work, looked as though we might do anything.

The trains delivered passengers to the station and after that they either had to walk or use horses for transport. There were no cars, a lot of horses that needed attention – feeding, rubbing down, moving to the stables, moving out of the stables and more. There weren't enough people to do the work. Again, many of the men had moved away to the bigger cities hoping for more money. I was offered a job without having to ask, more an order than a job offer.

Passing the local inn, a man shouted down at me from his saddle: 'Oi, you boy, take this horse to the stable, now!'

I knew nothing about horses. Jenna would have been better at this but equality wasn't on offer, they wanted a stable lad. I took the reins, the man jumped down, chucked me a coin, and disappeared.

'In 'ere,' an old man sitting on a stool waved me into the stable. 'Watch those back legs,' he laughed, seeing me jump after I'd led the horse into a stall. He had a lot more instructions. Most of them were to do with shovelling muck. I didn't finish until it was nearly dark.

Jenna came into the stable later and told me that the two of them were doing cleaning work in the inn. 'Not that Demelza does anything useful,' she added.

When I asked for my money the man laughed, 'They'll give you food.' He pointed to the inn. I was hungry enough not to argue. It was the same for the girls – food and a space to sleep but no wages. We were sat at a rickety table just outside the kitchen.

'What do we do now?' I sat back having eaten a pile of stale bread. I showed them the coin the horse rider had given me.

'I think it was called a farthing,' Demelza tossed it over in her hand. 'That's a quarter of an old penny and worth about nothing at all.'

Jenna left the table and went to talk to the landlord. I looked for more food. I pinched a small piece of pie sitting on a plate just inside the kitchen.

'Two more days' work and he'll get us the tickets,' Jenna grabbed the pie from me and ate the piece whole.

'You believe him?' I said, with my mouth open.

Jenna shrugged, the pie took some chewing. We did two more days. The landlord didn't want to do anything but keep us working. Jenna persuaded him that is was safer to let us go.

'What did you say to him?' I asked as we walked to the station.

'Not a lot,' she said, with a smile.

'She said you were a bit crazy and had killed several horses at your last job,' said Demelza. 'Horses or was it people?'

'Oh,' was all I could say and we walked on. The landlord had an arrangement at the station, it was the sort of 'arrangement' my dad might have had. But we did get tickets, and because the train wasn't full we even found seats, in something called third class, on a bench by ourselves.

'Just like home,' Jenna said, pointing towards the empty first class carriages.

'Better than looking after those horses,' I realised that no one was actually coming near me, even Jenna was keeping her distance. I suppose I was used to the smell. I sat back and relaxed in the space.

The train puffed out of the station and it almost felt like a holiday outing on one of those old railway lines until we realised that this was modern for the other passengers. They were saying how much better third class was now that they were allowed to be inside, not out in the rain which was almost constant anywhere around the moor. Soon the view from the grime streaked windows changed as we headed away from the high tors and past woodland and fields with cows and sheep. It stopped raining but there was still a lot of mud everywhere.

'Shut the window,' came an urgent shout and all the other passengers leapt to their feet to slam shut any lowered windows.

We were too slow. The train entered a tunnel, all the engine smoke blew back and filled our carriage; while still trying to close our window I was hit by a cloud of soot. Turning to the others as we came out into daylight again both Jenna and Demelza laughed at me.

'What?' I frowned.

Jen pointed to the long mirrors that were fixed above some of the seats. My blackened face stared out at me.

Unless the windows stayed open the stuffy air in the carriage was unbearable but we jumped when anyone else shouted to close them. I just had to wipe my face on my sleeve, which wasn't much cleaner. It wasn't just time tunnels that caused problems.

After a while we started to see more houses; small and grubby buildings at the side of the track, blackened by soot. The bench seat was getting hard to sit on by the time we pulled into the station – end of the line, and the search for Miss Tregarthur.

'Weird,' Jenna said, looking around the station. 'Looks like a normal place, you know, like station buildings in our time, just covered in soot.'

'And the horses outside,' I added as we walked out wondering which way to go.

We weren't going to take a horse and carriage because we had no idea where we would ask for and we had no money.

No idea where we were going. We wandered up a steep hill into the town. The first thing we saw was a huge church.

'The cathedral,' Demelza said.

'You'd know,' Jenna shoved her.

'What? Why?' Demelza stumbled.

'This was probably the place your priest came from,' Jenna shoved her again and she fell.

'Priest? What priest? I don't know any pri …' Demelza's face showed she remembered.

It had been Miss Tregarthur's plan to have us killed in the time of the Black Death, but not by the disease. They had sent for a priest, to help them decide exactly when was the right time to burn us to death.

Demelza's sorrys didn't work. Saying sorry for sending us to our death was never going to be enough. Jenna looked ready to carry out an execution of her own.

'Alvin, stop her,' Demelza looked up at me.

Jenna huffed and turned away. Demelza struggled to her feet with a sly look on her face. A sly look and a pout in my direction which she made sure Jenna saw.

'Are we really going to keep her with us?' I said quickly, Jenna said nothing and Demelza managed yet another pout. Impossible. This was her game and I felt helpless, something Demelza obviously understood. Something I rather hoped Jenna didn't understand.

It wasn't hard to find the trail of Miss Tregarthur. Even though this was quite a large town not a lot happened and anything different was noticed. People had noticed a wild looking woman arriving with someone called Masterson. Everyone seemed to know the name Masterson, a rich man who had another house and land just outside of the city.

We knew what we had to do and spent the rest of the day shifting horse dung, cleaning rooms and begging for food, which earned a night in a stable. The next day we set off to find Mr Masterson who, of course, lived in Masterson Hall.

We saw the Hall from perhaps more than a mile away as we trudged along a rutted gravel road, jumping out of the way of carriages which thundered down taking no notice of people trying to walk, and there were no pavements.

We were told that this was the main road to London – it wasn't a motorway. As we approached the Hall I can't say I felt confident. It was like his last house, but much larger. The place was vast and set in a park of huge trees with cows and sheep grazing underneath and men working everywhere. Whoever Masterson was, he must have had piles of money. We came to another gate, opening into the parkland. Two men stepped out in front of us blocking the way. Both in the same sort of uniform that we'd seen on the man outside his other house.

'No beggars,' said one of them.

The other was holding a pistol. He looked like he enjoyed turning people away.

I couldn't blame him, we looked really rough by now, three rough young kids, straw in my hair from the stables, the girls' clothing ragged and dirty. Jenna looked at me and burst out laughing which definitely confused the two men.

'Have you seen a crazy looking woman who looks like a witch with huge staring eyes and maybe screeches a bit?' Jenna said to the men after she'd stopped laughing at me.

It was obvious that the description fitted, they looked startled, a bit surprised but it was easy to see that they had seen Miss T – once seen never forgotten.

'Not your business,' the first one said, flustered by Jenna's question.

'Came to see your man Masterson didn't she?' Jenna added a bit of fierceness in her voice just in case she didn't get her own way.

'Gone to London,' the second man blurted out.

'Shut it John.' His companion turned on him. 'Just get these scum out of here or shoot them.'

John looked nervous and jumpy. He was the man with the gun. I really didn't like nervous jumpy men with guns. I'd seen men like that at home and Dad told me to watch out for them. 'Never know what they might do next,' he'd said, usually just before hitting them with his baseball bat. Mind you, he usually did that even if they weren't nervous or holding a gun.

That was Dad, a vicious drug runner now in jail – if 'now' meant the time we'd left home. As for the 'now' we were in, my dad hadn't even been born. Difficult to get my mind to work that out – we might be in trouble here but thinking of Dad made me wonder if I could get to him before he started a business that would get him, and me, into so much trouble.

A loud click brought me back to this particular present; John had readied his gun. I pulled Jenna and we turned away, Demelza followed quickly.

'And don't come back.' The first man grabbed the gun from John and fired it over our heads.

That made me stop. I could see that this gun had only one shot, it needed re-loading – John was fumbling with the barrel but it would take ages if they were going to shoot at us again.

They might be two guard men but I had Dad's temper in me and I didn't like the way they had spoken to us – perhaps this was my 'baseball bat' moment even though I only had my fists.

Jenna had hold of my arm and just shook her head saying: 'Miss Tregarthur's gone,' as she pulled me away and we walked away down the track.

'What now?' Demelza stuck in her whine after we'd walked a little way.

'Good question,' I couldn't see what we could do. Miss Tregarthur was just moving on, whatever she was doing we were just chasing her. Jenna didn't see this as a problem – going after her was what we had to do.

'We'll need a lot more money,' Jenna said, as we headed back towards the town. 'A lot more money if we are going to follow them to London.'

'Could use the …' I nodded towards my arm, where I still had the gold belt. I didn't want to let Demelza see it, no way I could trust her. She'd sell us out, probably find another 'Zach-like' person to steal the belt from me.

'Wait a minute,' Jenna grabbed hold of Demelza and spun her round. 'What have you got here?'

Jenna grabbed hold of the necklace that Demelza had worn ever since we first set out on the moor, the necklace we had spotted when she'd been held captive in the caveman village, and somehow she still had it hidden under the neck of her tunic. The fabric came apart in Jenna's grasp and the shivery metal shone in the sunlight.

'Leave it,' squealed Demelza and tears welled up in her eyes. 'It was my gran's.' Demelza croaked.

That stopped Jenna for maybe a second, before she undid the clasp and weighed the chain in her hand. Demelza sank to the ground, sobbing, 'It's all I have.'

Even with all the awful things that had happened, all down to Zach and Demelza, even after all that I could feel her misery. I understood. I had nothing from my family. If I ever did get home it looked like I'd have to live on the streets – with Dad in jail, Mum dead and the rest of the family not wanting me around.

The misery seemed to hit Jenna too and she handed the necklace over with no words. Demelza grabbed for it, looking surprised and bewildered as she fastened it around her neck again. Standing up, she turned to Jenna, 'Why?'

Jenna just shrugged and we set off back to the city. Something had changed and I didn't understand what had happened between the two of them. We still had work to do if we wanted our usual meal of bread and a night in a stinking hovel. Life as usual, that's what it had become. We'd have to sell the belt. I knew that would be difficult – too valuable. We didn't look like the legal owners of such a thing. Anyone would assume we'd stolen it and it would be difficult to find a king to back up our story. Trying to sell it would almost certainly see us end up in another jail.

'Maybe chop it up?' Jenna suggested, as we piled up some cleanish straw to make a sort of bed. Demelza had already slumped down in a corner.

'Sleep on it,' I murmured. I guessed that keeping it together made it a whole lot more valuable. Things changed after a restless, uncomfortable night.

-3-

NECKLACE

'She's gone.' Jenna woke me in the earliest light of morning, her voice disturbed the horses.

'Gone?' I said sleepily. The straw bed might be uncomfortable but the work to earn the place to sleep had been exhausting. I'd have gone back to sleep except Jen poked me and you don't sleep after her pokes.

'Do I care?' I muttered, and not just because I didn't see any use in keeping Demelza with us. There were other reasons I really had to keep out of my head. 'Has she taken anything?' I added, but we didn't have anything worth taking. Just another couple of coins from yesterday's jobs. At least in this inn we were paid in money, although we had to sleep in the stable.

Since we were awake, we made our way to the kitchen in the inn building, hoping to find more food. We just found more work.

'Get their horses,' the landlady called when she saw me and nodded towards two men who were eating an early breakfast. With a hungry sigh I did what she asked and brought the men's two horses round to the front of the building and stood there waiting for the landlord to bring their saddles and help the men leave with their heavy bags slung over the horses.

I went back into the inn for a crust before getting a list of jobs – nearly all involving horse dung – Jenna had more work since Demelza had left. We might be in the city but this place still didn't provide enough wealth to keep people from heading to larger places, including London.

Sleeping on the problem of selling the belt had made no difference. I was going to have to ask someone, to trust someone, perhaps the landlord. But looking at him I reckoned it would only be a minute or two after I told him before he found someone to take it from me. The idea was useless. We'd never get a good price for it. We might get enough money to get us to London, but not enough to survive when we got there. Working our way would take forever. We weren't going to find out what Miss T was up to and that worried me, her messing around in time, what would that do to all our futures? Especially mine, because I was the one she wanted to kill. But if we couldn't follow her, wasn't our only choice to head back to the moor?

I still thought Demelza knew more than she had told us. Something particular stuck in my head. Demelza had asked me if I knew Miss Tregarthur before we went with her on the first hike. I had no idea why she asked that. Something had happened such a long time ago. Hadn't I seen Miss Tregarthur hanging around my aunt's house? Perhaps I had been mistaken.

No point in asking Jenna about that now. She was struggling out of the inn with foul smelling chamber pots to empty into the open drain. No toilets and the filth just trickled down the drain, it wouldn't clear unless we had rain.

Jenna looked up, 'See the sign?' she said, looking up at the street name. 'Shitbrook.'

'Good name,' I wiped something off my boot.

'Back to the moor,' Jenna spat as she wiped her hand on her tunic, sniffed and pulled a face that would have exactly fitted her feelings and the smell.

I nodded. No future in staying here, only the past. We would never discover what Miss Tregarthur was up to and probably wouldn't even if we followed her to London. Just have to hope the tunnel would take us. If Demelza had left and she didn't have any money she would probably go back to the moor as well. It was even possible Demelza knew a lot more, perhaps she had remembered some way of getting the tunnel to take her.

Shouts came from inside the inn for us to get on with the work and we were about to walk away, when Demelza returned. More tears had streaked the dirt on her face. She said nothing and just handed Jenna a leather pouch which clinked of money.

Staring in a puzzled way I saw the line around her neck where the necklace had been. Demelza had sold the necklace. I didn't know how she'd done it but she'd got a good price. It wasn't a tiny pouch. Working in the inn gave us only a few coins, now we were almost rich. Should we let her try and sell the gold belt?

'Thanks, but why?' Jenna frowned.

Demelza just shook her head. Jen didn't ask again but she took charge and suggested to the landlady what she might do with her dirty chamber pots.

'Clothes,' Jenna said. 'We need to blend in.'

At the time I did blend in quite well – dirt and smell were fashionable for boys looking after horses.

'First a bath,' Jenna led us off to another inn, not a great place – it still had chamber pots which Jenna kept on calling for someone to empty – but we got a bath, just one and I was the last in the water. In a cleaner and less disgusting state we went looking for new clothes. We weren't after anything too posh, second hand stuff. I ended up with a black woollen jacket with a waistcoat and trousers. I'd seen old photographs of people looking like this. Along with a pair of heavy boots. Both the girls were in smock dresses. Jenna always looked great to me. Trouble was, Demelza didn't look bad either, and she knew it, swirling around with a smile that suggested the necklace and her gran were probably forgotten.

The new clothes we had were not something I would want to be seen in at home in our time.

'Jen, you really do look great,' Demelza said unexpectedly and I couldn't understand why Jenna seemed to take it as an insult.

I tried not to notice Demelza.

I couldn't understand why she'd sold her necklace. Why did she care if we went after Miss Tregarthur? If the crystal didn't work anymore we were at the mercy of the time tunnel, it might help or more likely it wouldn't.

I could only guess Demelza thought finding Miss Tregarthur was the best way of getting home, not necessarily along with me and Jen. I didn't feel that Demelza had suddenly turned into a good guy, selling her family necklace and giving us the money. Perhaps I was too harsh, perhaps we'd never know and at least we weren't broke. Even so, if we went to London we'd still need more money. This gold belt around my arm felt definitely more of a problem than a solution.

I still had a feeling I was missing out on information from

both of the girls. When we had arrived at the moor this time and after we'd dumped Zach in the tunnel something had happened, Jenna knew more and hadn't shared it. Same for Demelza and getting anything out of her was … well … difficult. If I went near her Jenna started bristling like one of Dad's attack dogs.

All I could guess was that Demelza must have had a good reason for selling her gran's necklace and it would be for her benefit. Did the necklace ever really belong to her grandmother? Demelza looked at me as though she read my mind, and gave the sort of smile I was glad Jenna didn't see.

We had a real meal that night. It was so long since I had sat down with some real food in front of me – even though it wasn't food I'd have eaten at home, not that I actually knew what we were eating – a lump of meat was the main thing we hacked at and ate with bread. Even Demelza chopped off a greasy hunk and sat back with a small dribble of fat running down her face. The sort of sequence you wouldn't want anyone else to see – especially since Demelza had once been so careful with her appearance. Again she gave me a look that suggested she knew what I was thinking and slowly wiped her face keeping her eyes on me. Jenna grunted and she might have said something about my needing to shut my mouth.

Being a more up-market place, this inn had a more up-market class of criminal. You could spot them at the bar, furtive, not the pickpockets that had been everywhere out on the streets. In here they were plotting and I had a feeling that we might be part of the plot. Being cleaner, we looked younger and like potential victims. We were out of place and certainly out of time.

We went up to our room soon after the meal. Upstairs we had one bed for all three of us to stretch out on as best we could. Demelza winked at me and got into the middle. Jenna shoved her over to the side.

The inn creaked with noise. People still drinking.

'Eh?' I said, as Jenna shoved past Demelza, got up and pulled a chair across the room to the door.

'No lock,' she said, in a loud whisper.

'Oh,' I said, as she jammed the chair under the door handle.

We were too exhausted to worry any more. Demelza snored, not surprising after that meal, but soon I was asleep.

Not for long – I woke to hear the door knob turn and rub against Jenna's chair. The room was dark, just a flickering lamp outside in the street. I didn't think the chair would stay in place so I jumped up and held it.

'Smash it down,' I heard a man's voice.

'Jonah said no noise,' came another voice.

'They're only kids aren't they?' the other man said. 'Give the door a hard push.'

'Alvin,' Jenna's voice sounded loud in the dark. 'Alvin, is the gun loaded?'

She sounded so serious that I almost believed her and half turned to see if she did have a gun. Difficult not to laugh when I realised what she meant. I made some noises which I hoped sounded gun like.

'Pass me the shot,' I called.

There was silence outside the door, the sound of footsteps leaving. We took it in turns to keep watch after that, but we weren't disturbed again. We left the inn early next morning – the landlord's name was Jonah so he must have known about the men who tried to get into our room. I suspected he wouldn't care how much noise they made in the day if they were going to rob us – or worse.

We set off down to the train station to travel to London. If we had no idea what this man Masterson and Miss T were up to, would we ever find them? I didn't think it would be so easy in the city. We had to hope Mr Masterson was famous enough for us to find him. What were we going to do if we did catch up with them? Jenna seemed more certain but I wasn't sure what she was certain about.

Demelza had done well selling the necklace so we bought tickets for second class. Might even have enough to get us back. We had time to talk as we waited on the platform.

'If Miss Tregarthur believes the tunnel has taken her to the wrong time, what is she going to do?' I looked to Jenna for an answer although I actually believed Demelza might have a better idea.

'Maybe she's worked out an idea about getting the crystal to work again.' Jenna turned to Demelza. 'You got any idea?'

Demelza words were not loud enough to overcome the steam and hooting noise of our train arriving. The whole station filled with steam.

We took the train on a warm morning, in July 1883 as I found out. The journey took us from the countryside to the town, almost a time travel journey itself, moving past villages and towns that were so different to those we had seen around the moor. Time didn't change but the world appeared more modern as we headed for the capital.

On the journey there was time to think and talk again, even if we did have to shut the windows at each tunnel – this train hooted every time to give a warning. I was trying to decide how to ask my questions. I had the feeling that neither of the girls wanted to share things. So much thinking soon made me drift off, this second class carriage was quite comfortable. We had a small compartment with a corridor outside running along the train. Room for six people but the train wasn't full so we had the space to ourselves.

It looked like pictures you see of old trains – well, of course it was an old train, actually a new old train – changing time is impossible. What was it that had brought us here? We had called it a tunnel, although it was nothing like these soot filled railway tunnels. It changed, at first part of the rock, and we'd had to move piles of stones to find it, then it became more like a gas that swirled around and drew us in. The last time there were spaces – maybe caves or something – inside it.

'What is this tunnel?' Demelza said suddenly. Maybe I had been mumbling my thoughts aloud.

'What do you mean?' Jenna snapped.

'This time travel thing, it's alive, ok?'

I said nothing, hoping Demelza would give us some more information. She'd been with Alice Tregarthur for … well it could be thousands of years if you started in the time of mammoths like we did.

'But what does that mean, what sort of thing is it?' Demelza was fishing for information.

Jenna looked away but I felt she did know more.

It was my time for a, 'What?' and that had lots of question marks with it.

'COME ON, tell me,' I shouted when neither of them said any more.

Jenna gave a huff: 'The crystal Miss Tregarthur uses to control the tunnel. I told you, we have to get it back, it's part of whatever it is.'

'You found out more when we carried Zach into it?' I had to know even if Demelza was going to find out.

'Yeah.' Jenna paused. 'It was sort of speaking to me but without words, just sounds in my head. Made me feel I was going crazy, still does, but …'

'But what?' I said quickly as we slowed for another station.

Jenna was struggling with her words but went on: 'It feels as though there is something inside the rocks. I don't know what it is. It almost feels like a person. This crystal is part of its heart. It cannot live without it.'

'A real person? Stuck inside?' I said, with a shiver.

'I don't know, I just don't know,' Jenna winced. 'I could feel the pain and anger coming from the rock. Each time Miss Tregarthur hit the crystal the pain got worse.'

Jenna's face told me how hard this had been and I waited to see if she was going to put that into words.

'I couldn't take it,' Jen blurted. 'I couldn't stand to hear, to feel, that pain. We just have to get this crystal back.'

'But the crystal is dead, it's dead, isn't it?' Demelza looked at me, at Jen and back. 'Isn't it? Why would it want a dead crystal? It's hopeless, we're stuck here forever. I'm stuck here forever with you two.' She buried her head in her hands, very dramatically; Demelza was good at drama.

Did it matter what state the crystal was in, as Demelza had said? Jenna didn't know the answer. I couldn't cope with the idea of a dead or alive piece of stone.

Demelza's drama seemed even more false than usual. Did Miss Tregarthur know another way to get the crystal to work again? If she did, then Demelza might know the same thing. Was that what Miss Tregarthur was doing?

Questions, no answers.

The train stopped and more people got on. Two men came into our compartment and sat talking about machines and whether there would be a war. I was going to ask more questions but Jen shook her head and we stayed quiet until we reached the end of this journey. London arrived with smoke and a smell worse than ever. The train pulled into Waterloo. I'd been there, Waterloo, London. I'd gone on a visit with Mum as a young kid.

-4-

LONDON

The noise of London hit us as we left the station. Streets packed with horse drawn carriages, rumbling and rattling over cobbles. Horses pulling everything from buses to overloaded carts, their drivers standing up to shout and wave their fists as they tried to push through impossibly small spaces. Carts carrying fruit, some stacked high with furniture, many with large signs advertising impossible claims: medicines that cured everything; lotion to restore bald hair, milk that made babies more perfect.

Piles of fresh and steaming horse dung littering the road. This was a town of horses. The air a haze of soot and smoke. An overwhelming smell of overloaded drains.

Once we saw a car – broken down. A car that looked ancient.

'Like … from a museum,' Jenna said.

'Looks like it's headed to one now,' I said, seeing the steam coming from the bonnet. People had gathered around to stare, the men on horses to shout insults.

On the pavements, business men hurried in dark suits and round topped hats, women in long dresses and always hats and bonnets, even the working men wore jackets and flat caps. Boys selling fruit, girls selling flowers, women selling baskets, men looking shifty.

Finding an inn in this mess of noise and smell was difficult. Near the station we found more than one hotel much too big and a bit scary for us. We headed to the river, crossing a bridge with the stench rising from the brown scummed water, busy with barges and boats. We walked for ages to a cheaper part of town with narrower and dirtier streets, buildings crowded together bulging over the roads. Eventually we found an inn that would take us, not necessarily the safest place. The large fat landlord took our money and called for a girl to show us the room.

'Can't do the stairs,' he pointed at his leg and limped away.

No one at the inn had heard of a Mr Masterson or seen anyone like Miss T – although there were pretty strange people all around. Asking questions made us stand out. We definitely weren't in a posh part of town. I said Masterson was loaded – or at least Jenna translated 'loaded' into words the men in the inn understood. They laughed at us and said the place to find him would be in the expensive business area called the City, even though I thought that meant the whole of London. But the City was a small area of London where all the money dealings went on. Not the sort of place the three of us would belong.

'It'll all be men,' Jenna suggested the next day and so I went off alone and left the other two behind.

My clothes gave me away as someone from the country and people kept shouting insults at me. That made me feel like a target for anyone who might rip me off. I had to ask directions but I kept moving when they tried to stop me and ask questions. I had nothing I wanted to explain.

As I neared the City area the shops looked old and quaint and more expensive, some sold jewellery. Maybe it would be easier to sell the gold belt here. But only easier for someone who didn't feel so out of place, vulnerable. Selling gold could really land me in trouble here. I walked on. Wondering what to do. How to find one man in this city? Simple in the end.

I wandered about for ages, walking quickly to pretend I had somewhere to go. The roads dotted with horse manure made it easy for someone to put a foot wrong, which was something for everyone to stop and laugh at.

The city buildings were huge grand places – they looked like buildings I had seen in my own time when I'd been to London. But the smell of soot lingered everywhere, even here where the streets were cleaner.

Around me everyone looked busy, smartly dressed money men going in and out of the buildings, talking to each other, it was all about money. Despite my hurrying, I soon felt everyone was staring at me.

I asked a few people about Masterson but no one took me seriously, they just laughed at me, told me to 'go home, country boy'. I decided to leave, go back and get Jenna, we'd be better wandering around together. Although the people looking busy were all men there were couples walking together. Women with parasols even though the sun only shone faintly. Long dresses which looked really impractical with all the horse dung about.

I really did not fit in. I could have done better if I had a barrow selling something – hot chestnuts seemed to be doing well. I thought Jenna would do better at asking questions. Most women didn't go into the buildings but there were working women on the street gathered around stalls selling flowers, and fruit and more baskets. Men dressed in working clothes flitted between the stalls; dodgy looking men. This looked like a great place for pickpockets.

A man came out onto the street. Striding out with purpose he put up a stall and shouted something over and over. He wasn't one of the money men, he was selling newspapers. I went closer to try and hear what he was shouting, a crowd was gathering near him, anxious people wanting to buy his papers. I caught his words:

'Masterson to buy the Heath. Masterson to buy Hampstead Heath.'

I was jostled out of the way by people rushing for papers and talking about this piece of news. Hampstead Heath, I knew that was some park in London. I'd been there with Granddad, so many years ago, before the worst of the trouble at home. Although years ago still meant years ahead of the time I was in. Hampstead Heath was a big green space, we'd kicked a ball around, walked up some hill, he'd bought me a cake in a café there. What on earth did anyone want to buy the place for? This had to be due to Miss Tregarthur, but what would she want with this park? I wasn't the only one asking that question. All the money men were puzzled and there was soon a loud noise of arguing voices:

'Will they let him?'

'Can't do it, public park, he can't do it.'

'It's ours, stop him.'

'Money will do anything,' one man said loudly and that caused a pause in the chatter but it soon took up again with voices becoming angrier. I wandered away still hearing some of the conversation:

'He'll lose all his money,' I heard one smart suited man say to another. 'Nothing he can do with it. Messy place, lot of swamps aren't there?'

That was odd because when I went there with Granddad it had been surrounded by houses, part of London. Perhaps London was a lot smaller. I needed to get back to the others.

'Worthless now,' said Jenna, when I told her about the Heath. 'But worth a fortune in our time. Maybe that's what she's doing, trying to make a pile of money for the future.'

'Got to be an easier way to do that with time travel,' Demelza joined in; I supposed making money was something she and Zach had planned.

'How?' I asked.

'Find out the result of the lottery, then go back and win it.' Demelza certainly had this idea sorted. I thought there might be problems with getting back to the exact right time. There could be loads of things to bet on here but we had no idea of the results.

'Has to be more than just making money,' Jenna said. 'What do they use this Heath place for in our time?'

'It's just a park,' I told them about the time I'd been there with my grandfather. It was hard for me to talk about him, to talk about anything good in my family. I noticed Demelza rub her neck as I talked – must have been remembering her gran and the necklace. Had it been worth selling that? Jenna said Demelza was like a toy that had lost its stuffing or lost any connection with our world and her own family. Did I care? Demelza had it coming. She had changed since selling it, at least she had stopped pretending to flirt with me, made my time much easier.

We carried on talking about what Miss Tregarthur might have been up to and got nowhere.

'Did you think I knew Miss Tregarthur before this all started?' It seemed the right time for me to ask Demelza.

'Must have?' she stopped.

'Why?' There was more to this. I looked at Jenna. Did she know more?

'Tell me,' I shouted.

'We don't know for certain.' Jenna bit her lip.

'Know what?'

'Miss T might have said you were part of her family,' Demelza said slowly.

My mouth opened without words.

'Her family is tied up with this time tunnel thing, this crystal.' Demelza stopped again.

'Do you remember where you lived when you were younger?' Jenna sounded scared to ask.

'No, not really, moved about a lot,' I stuttered. Did I remember? A sort of flashback came into my head; that moor again. Had I been there before? I hadn't felt that I recognised anything when we first went out on the moor.

'You found the time tunnel,' Demelza said, meaning the first time at the start of this disastrous trip, starting with the storm and the ground shaking.

'I ...' I thought I'd just stumbled in the earthquake. Stumbled into the cave with that light.

'And led us all through?' Jenna said it as though it was a question.

'All my fault?' This was making me angry.

'No, but you may be more linked to this mess than you know.'

Jenna tried to calm me down, before changing the subject: 'We've got to go and take a look at this park. There has to be more to this than just the land. Time to go.'

'Got a bus map?' I snapped. I could see that Jenna and Demelza might not know a lot more, but I felt that they had guessed more and probably talked about it without me. I wasn't sure I wanted to know if I was part of that awful woman and her family. We'd met some of them and they weren't people I wanted to meet again. Except Mum. How had she really got mixed up with this? She was dead now, surely? Was there more history about Mum and the Tregarthurs?

While I was tossing ideas around in my head we waited in the road. I'd asked the landlord at the inn how we might find a carriage.

'Did you find your Masterson?' he had asked me.

I shook my head, surprising that he should remember the name. He knew nothing about Masterson when I asked him before. Asking questions wasn't always a great idea.

'Just wait by the road outside, carriage should come along before long.' He turned to his bar, he was a man who did more drinking than work. His limp became more obvious whenever he was called to do something.

He was right. Soon a horse drawn open carriage pulled up. Jenna negotiated a price to take us to Hampstead Heath.

'Long way,' said a one-armed man, who sat up by the driver, the one doing the negotiating and a man I wouldn't trust, but Jenna climbed up to the carriage and the three of us were soon bouncing along the streets. I wondered if the landlord had fixed this particular carriage for us.

Much later, we were out of the city into woodland, a sign

said Camden which was near where Granddad had lived. Few houses here now. Eventually we came out into a clearing; we'd passed a sign saying Hampstead village. Further on, a wooded hill stretched out in front of us, this had to be the Heath.

'Not a lot of swamp,' I said.

'That's over the hill,' called the driver's mate. Again I had a bad feeling about him but he went on. 'Walk up there and you can see the whole of London.' He pointed to a large notice nailed to one of the trees up the hill out on the Heath, near it a group of men were working. 'That'll tell you all about the Heath.'

We climbed down to the road.

'Don't all have to go,' the man called from his seat. 'Let the girls stay here if you want.'

I felt uneasy, the driver and his mate didn't feel right.

But Jen was saying, 'Come on,' and took off towards the sign.

Demelza hung back. She didn't fancy the walk, too muddy.

'Ok love,' the man said. 'You can stay in the carriage and wait for them. Won't take long.'

Did I worry about what could happen to Demelza? I set off after Jenna. I didn't think Jenna wanted me to be too concerned about Demelza.

The park sign just told us a bit about the park and loads of rules. Apparently thousands of people came up here, there'd been parties and all sorts of problems with the crowds. Didn't say anything about it being for sale.

Over at one side there were a group of workmen building a fence. It wasn't on the main part of the Heath.

We went over to the men, planning to ask, but they soon shouted at us to get away. There was a sign on a nearby tree saying the 'Masterson Tregarthur Company' had bought it.

The other thing the sign said was 'Keep out'.

It looked like they were trying to buy land near to the Heath even if they couldn't get the whole thing – why? It was a scrubby piece of land, nothing there. Maybe Jenna was right, it was the sort of place that would cost a fortune to buy in our real time. But there had to be more to this.

'Whatever she wants it for, those men are trying to stop anyone finding out,' Jenna said, as we turned away.

As we walked back down the hill there was a fantastic view of London stretching down to the river. A thick cloud of smog lay over the town but you could still make out some of the sights.

'Isn't that St Paul's Cathedral?' I said pointing. It was another part of London that Granddad had shown me.

Jenna shrugged. 'Could be. You certainly can look down on the town from up here. Still no idea what she wants this place for except the view.' Jenna took one more glance up the hill before we made for the coach.

We were still a way off when we saw the struggle. Demelza was trying to get out of the carriage. She gave a scream as the man pulled her back with his hand over her mouth.

'RUN,' shouted Jenna and she charged across the rough grass.

We both ran. The driver flicked his whip and the horse took off. Panting, we arrived at the empty road with the carriage disappearing, Demelza still struggling uselessly.

I wasn't sure I really cared if Demelza had been kidnapped – if that's what had happened, but I just knew Jenna wouldn't see it that way.

I felt it couldn't be a complete coincidence that we should be singled out. We might look like country people, that wasn't enough, how would anyone know we were here? The only person who would take any notice was Miss Tregarthur, surely she couldn't have spotted us or seen me – unless it was my asking around in the city. Had someone told her or told Masterson?

'What do they want her for?' I asked because Jenna wasn't saying anything.

'I don't like to imagine that,' Jenna said in the end. 'Reminds me what happened on those convict boats to Australia.'

Another awful time in history that Miss Tregarthur had sent us to, along with me having to escape a sentence to hang.

'But …' I stammered, not wanting to ask anymore. I had never asked Jenna what she'd had to do to survive that journey, the time when Ivy ended up with a baby and we'd left them behind.

'But what?' Jenna snapped and I think she was just remembering what had happened.

'But …' I had nothing more to say.

'But nothing,' Jenna was going to say what I expected. 'We've got to find her.'

-5-

Lost Girl

If finding Demelza was going to be difficult, so was getting back to the inn. We were not exactly on a bus route. Any horse drawn private carriages hurried past us taking passengers to the city. From the hill up on the Heath we'd been able to see over the town so we had a rough idea of which direction to take, but we hadn't paid attention to the route before. We set off and we weren't exactly in the middle of anything like a town, there was still a lot of countryside around here – in this part of the century.

After a while we were amongst the houses and couldn't work out where we were going.

'Make for the smell,' Jenna sniffed. 'The worst smell comes from the river, the inn's not far from there.'

I wasn't sure I could detect where the worst smell came from, but Jen was walking faster so I kept up and hoped she knew where to go. She didn't. Ages later we stopped and asked someone. I'd thought that was useless, the inn was called the Red Lion, a common name. But asking worked, because people knew of the big landlord with a limp – big in terms of the size of his beer belly, limp in terms of when he decided to use it. The expression on their faces made me worry even more. Our landlord had a long history.

We made it back. It was clear that someone had been in our room and not just to empty the chamber pot. They must have been disappointed because we didn't have anything to steal. Demelza had handed over the money from the sale of the necklace and Jen kept it with her and there wasn't a lot of it left.

We went down to the bar to ask a few questions. The landlord seemed to be waiting for us. But he had no answers when we asked him about our room, he said it often happened.

'There's a lot of thieving people around, can't keep them out,' he sneered at us. This was going nowhere. The landlord was pretending to line up bottles, probably the most strenuous thing he'd done all day – relying on his wife and a young girl who was pushing a broom around the bar room without much effect, this inn really needed a team of contract cleaners with a power hose.

'Oh, I forgot,' said the fat limping man and it didn't sound as though he'd forgotten anything. 'Man dropped this off for you.'

He handed me a scrap of paper, the whole thing felt fake. The note was a demand for money if we wanted to see Demelza again. Actually I didn't but that was never going to be Jenna's reaction when I passed her the note.

'What man?' Jenna said loudly.

'No idea,' the landlord said again with his sneering voice.

Now Jen is a wonderful person, caring, loving but she hasn't always been like that. Back at school she'd been as hard – harder – than anyone. No one messed with Jenna at home. This trip may have changed her, but not completely.

'Last chance,' Jenna said sweetly.

The landlord gave a jeering laugh and turned his back on

her, but not for long. Jenna snatched the broom from the girl and with a yell started to smash anything in reach – bottles from the bar, kicking over the chairs and tables, and finally throwing one of the chairs through a window.

'Hey,' shouted the slowly moving man with his face an angry snarl, his fat arms making to grab my Jen.

I'm not so caring and loving. And I might still be quite young, even if I did feel older, but our last Tregarthur time trip on the boats had changed me. I'd been at sea for months, running up the rigging, hard physical work, better than a gym work out. So this man wasn't as scary as he might have been. As he lumbered towards us I stuck a chair out in from of him. I don't suppose he really saw it over his belly, but it was enough to trip him. And I followed Dad's advice – never put a man on the ground and watch to see what he does next because you won't like it, follow through. I grabbed one of the bottles Jenna had broken and jumped on top of him, squashing the final bits of puffing breath he had. And when he had stopped gasping for air I had the broken glass stuck firmly at his neck. There are some skills you might not want to learn from your dad, but this one turned out to be pretty handy.

Now the landlord's reinforcements were arriving. Two big men were at the door, not the two from the carriage, these two were different and dangerous.

'Fred,' one of them called to the landlord and took a step towards us.

'Alvin, cut his throat.' Jenna stepped in front of the new man, who looked confused at being challenged by her. But I got the message and pushed the broken glass harder, blood trickled down the man's neck.

'No!' squealed Fred, I hadn't known his name before. 'Stay back, stay back, they'll kill me,' he squealed again.

'Not back,' Jenna demanded, 'OUT. Get out or we'll do him.'

Jenna's voice even frightened me.

'Do what she says,' Fred snivelled and the other two men left. I was sure I heard one of them give a laugh. I don't think there was much friendship between this lot, probably they'd have been happy if I had killed Fred.

Left alone in the room I could see this wasn't going to be easy, not easy to keep this big man under control.

'Tell us what really happened,' Jenna tried to sound firm, but I could hear uncertainty in her voice now, uncertainty and quite a bit of fear.

'Sure,' replied Fred gaining confidence and slyness sounding in his words. He might be fat and lazy but he must have dealt with many bar fights in this part of the town. 'Just let me up and I'll tell you all about it, sort things out,' he said, and moved slightly as though he might get up.

I pushed harder with the broken bottle and he gave a cry.

'No need for that,' he cried. 'I'll help you.'

I cut off his words with another jab of the bottle and another trickle of blood.

'Pull his trousers down,' I called to Jenna, remembering another trick Dad had told me. Jenna did as I asked, despite the unwashed whiff and the lack of any underpants. A man with his trousers around his knees finds it hard to get away.

'Give me his belt.' I held one hand out behind me, still ready with the bottle in my other hand. But I needed Jen to fasten the belt around Fred's neck. With that in place I could hold him and pull hard if he tried to escape. I pulled him up to his knees. His angry face stared at us, but he tried to cover his undressed state as Jenna stood over him.

'We could have found our way back here by smelling him,' Jenna said to me and I could tell she was rehearsing just to make sure the uncertainty wasn't still in her voice. It wasn't. 'Now Fred,' she went on. 'Do tell us about this,' she said, holding up the note.

Fred tried again to get himself up. I tightened the belt. His hands jerked to his neck but I had my foot on his back and he couldn't fight me and sank down on his knees.

'Don't do that again,' Jenna took another of the bottles she had smashed. 'I'm not good with this, never know where to strike, especially with you down there and no pants.'

Fred gave a moan. 'You've done this before,' he choked.

'Of course,' Jenna said, convincingly enough for me to almost try and remember when we had done this before.

After a lot more choking, more blood, a bit more shouting and a lot of threats, we left the inn with the information he'd given us. I didn't believe most of it, because it made Fred sound as though he'd been forced to help the others kidnap Demelza, but it was more likely he was involved from the start. And I could tell there was something he wasn't going to tell us even if I had done more damage with the broken glass. We were going to have to find out for ourselves, if we could.

The only possibly useful thing Fred had told us was that the man who owned the carriage and his driver both drank at a tavern down by the river – a pub to me – called the Captain Kidd. I thought he had told the truth about that because it would be easy for Fred to sort things out if we turned up there. Probably the pub was run by someone he knew.

There was plenty of time for Fred to get a message to the other two. Everything felt just as dangerous as anything Miss Tregarthur had done to us. We had tied Fred's belt to a rail on the bar before we left. It wouldn't hold him for long.

Jenna stood over Fred. 'You've been so helpful,' she said, with her own sneer. 'When we meet up with those other two we'll have to tell them just how helpful, how you said this was all their idea. How you said you'd say that in a law court, all their fault.'

I could see that was working on the barman's brain, he screwed up his eyes, so much hate on his face. But he could see that Jenna's threat made sense. It wouldn't do for him to be found to have grassed on the other men. It might not stop Fred in the end, but perhaps it would stop him for a while.

'And we'll tell them how a girl got the better of you and pulled down your pants.'

I joined Jenna with a laugh. What we really needed, and didn't have, was a phone with a camera. The threat of posting his picture in that state would have been a better threat. But no phones around.

I held on to Fred while Jenna got the few things we had from our room. We left, taking a quick turn down an alleyway and looking back to see if we were followed. Even from a distance away we could hear Fred's swearing and shouting. Time to run even if that made us look more suspicious. I didn't know exactly where we were going but made sure we took lots of narrow turns trying to keep roughly in the direction I had taken in the morning. I hoped that would take us to a more expensive part of the city, less likely that Fred's lot would follow us. I must have taken the wrong direction. We ended up near another station.

Eventually we found another inn that was a bit less rough. I could see they weren't too happy to have us but I guess the place needed the business and they gave us a room. They wanted money up front. It might be expensive but maybe there was less chance of us getting robbed.

One night was going to take nearly all the rest of our money and I wasn't certain we'd get the full use of the hotel. We were going to have to wait until night to meet up with the other men in the Captain Kidd.

'Police?' Jenna said, as we looked around the inn, checking for escape routes, just in case. 'Are there any police?' I hadn't seen anyone who looked like the police in this part of town. There had been some in the City near the banks, but nothing here.

'Maybe,' I said, after a while in silence but we both knew that even if we did find the police we'd have to do a lot of explaining. What would we say about Demelza, who was Demelza? Lost schoolgirl? Demelza didn't look like one, she'd looked a wreck even in the new clothes we'd bought.

'Worse than a tramp,' Jenna said, and I could see there was something else in her mind. Something she wasn't going to tell me right then. At least we could laugh about Fred and the mess we'd left for him. Would future guests in his inn be in the same danger? I wanted to hope that we could have made a difference, frightened him a bit, but that was a ridiculous thought. I'm sure Dad would have felt the same.

'So, we go down to the Captain Kidd, find these men and ask them nicely to hand over Demelza.' Jenna slumped onto the bed and sunk into the tired mattress which gave up a cloud of dust. This inn might be better, but total comfort was not on offer. 'That's just not going to work,' Jenna added.

'No,' I replied seeing that Jen expected me to come up with a better idea, any idea. 'We go down there and watch.'

'How?' Jenna was sliding into a hopeless mood. It made me wonder if we should bother about Demelza or just leave her. But looking at Jen made me almost feel as though her words and her mood were just a trap for me. Jen was expecting me to say we should leave her, but that's not what she wanted. And because of how I felt about Jenna I had to try harder. I also thought this whole thing might have been arranged for us and that meant arranged by Miss Tregarthur. Finding Demelza could lead us to her.

'This place is all fog and smoke,' I said. 'If we get a carriage we can sit outside the Captain Kidd and wait for them. They won't see us. We can follow them.'

Jenna wasn't convinced. 'Can we afford that? Another carriage?'

'Ah, I may be able to help with that,' I said, putting my hand into my breeches pocket. 'I decided Fred owed us more than the lies he gave us. So I removed what he had in his own trousers before we left. He kept the inn's takings on him – didn't trust to put them anywhere else.' I spread the coins on the bed beside her.

'Should be enough for a little night time surveillance,' I said. 'At least we'll be able to recognise one of them.' I was thinking about his one arm.

'Better make sure we know where we are now.' Jenna looked out of the window. 'The White Hart, we need to know where it is. Don't want to get lost like last time.'

'That's if we do come back here,' I said, imagining all the things that were likely to go wrong. Coming back with Demelza was one of them.

That night we did find another carriage. I spent a while talking to the driver. I didn't entirely explain what had happened, just what we wanted to do. It took nearly all of Fred's inn money to get an agreement with him. I gave him half and promised the rest if it all worked out.

'Can we trust him?' Jenna whispered after we climbed into the wooden coach and sat on the hard seats. This was a closed carriage, we needed to stay hidden.

'Of course we can't trust him,' I replied and we bumped off along the rutted road heading for the river. 'It'll be a money thing. If the driver reckons he can get more by dumping us in it, then he will. We just have to hope.'

'Do I get to pull down his trousers too?' Jen tried to laugh but we were out of humour.

It was difficult to know we had arrived as the driver pulled his horse to a stop. Along the road gas lamps shone in hazy globes, hanging in the thick fog, but too weak to light the ground. Dark thick choking fog. The driver pointed out the Captain Kidd.

'You want to go inside?' he asked.

'No, we'll wait for them,' Jenna called back.

The man shrugged and pulled a blanket round him. It felt cold in the damp air. We sat and waited. And waited. I could hear the driver was getting fed up, he kept asking if it wouldn't be best for us to go inside. 'Warmer in there,' he said, and I could see he wanted to get off, no matter how much we'd paid him for the night.

The fog drifted past in sheets of white against the gas lights, hiding everything as it went by but clearing for some brief seconds to let us see down the cobbled lane. Jenna and I were huddled down inside the carriage and didn't see the two men, but we heard them when they eventually left the inn.

'Found him with his trousers down,' was the first thing I heard.

I peered out but still couldn't see anyone clearly, it was obviously our two men because they went on to tell more of the story than I would have expected Fred to have wanted them to know; about how we had run off with the money. As I listened the two men came briefly into sight as they walked past our carriage. I could see the man with one arm. Ours was not the only carriage waiting outside the Captain Kidd. Several had queued up, presumably to collect drinkers at the end of their session. But our two men crossed the road and made for their own carriage. The one in which we'd travelled to the Heath. I hadn't recognised it, nothing to make it recognisable.

But in a brief clear moment I saw the driver pull the nose bag from the horse, swing himself up onto the cab and they set off, not very steadily. They had been in the inn for a long time. I had to hope that drink would make following them a bit safer, less noticeable. I called to our driver.

''Bout time,' he called back with a shiver and we were off.

Their carriage continued to weave about the road, meeting shouts from other drivers. We were heading into the main part of town. After a while it was clear we were moving into a more expensive area. Larger houses with their own lights outside.

'Better smelling too,' said Jenna.

'You want me to go on?' our driver called down and sounded nervous. Perhaps this wasn't a part of town to be caught following people. We followed them into a side street and this definitely wasn't so posh. The road had an empty dangerous feel to it. We weren't too far away from the river but the fog was less thick and we could easily see the other carriage pull up outside a well-lit house. It wasn't the only carriage. There was a noise of singing in the air, the sound of a piano.

'I'm not hanging around here.' Our driver climbed down and opened our door. 'You can pay me for this and I'll be off.'

'What's so wrong here?' I asked.

The man pointed at the house. 'If you find your girl in that place, then she's in trouble.'

I hadn't explained about Demelza to the driver, but he would have overheard Jenna and me talking. I still couldn't see what the problem was with this house.

Two women came out, supporting or half carrying a man. From their clothes it was pretty clear what was happening.

'It's a brothel,' Jenna confirmed what was obvious. 'They've taken her there. Probably sold her.'

If I had been alone I might have left with our driver, but Jenna persuaded me. Or at least held on to me just in case I might leave. I couldn't see any way we could get into this house with any safety.

Until Jenna said, 'Staggering time.'

Jenna took hold of me and we lurched out across the road.

I had no idea what she was up to but followed her lead as we heard our carriage disappear.

'Drunk and looking for fun,' Jenna said loudly in my ear just before we barged through the door and without hesitation Jenna winked at the two big men guarding the place and said, 'Room please, I need to get some money from this country lad.'

They laughed and pointed to a door. I realised from our last trip that Jenna had probably learnt a lot from her time on the convict boats, and maybe even more from pretending to be one of the prostitutes when she went to visit Demelza on the prison hulks. Possibly learnt a bit too much.

Falling in drunken fashion through the door we found ourselves in the tiny room. Empty, except for the bed and a small table laid out with a messy mixture of powders and puffs.

'What now?' I suggested.

Jenna raised her eyebrows. 'Don't you remember anything that Mrs Wilks told us in Sex-Ed?'

-6-

The Idea

This didn't all go to plan, mostly because there wasn't really a plan, just Jenna's idea. And we weren't really some sort of secret agents, just Jenna and me.

'We need to find out where she is before we do it,' Jenna said, and she hadn't really explained what the 'it' was. But I wasn't asking because of her previous comment. After which, despite being in a mess and in the wrong century Jenna had collapsed in laughter on the bed.

'You looked so scared,' she said, in between hiccupped laughs.

I didn't reply. When she had finished poking fun at me about Miss Wilks' lessons – which were as bizarre as school Sex-Ed can get – she told me her idea.

This small room they'd let us have must have been used by other women to do their makeup ready for work. Jenna really had learnt a lot when she had visited Demelza on the prison ships. Learnt from the other girls she met.

'That's how I knew about getting a room,' Jen explained. 'The girls on the ship used to pick up a man and they didn't have anywhere of their own so they'd bring them to a place like this. Rent a room – they'll expect you to pay,' Jenna laughed again.

'Oh,' was about all I could say. Jenna hadn't told me the whole story of what happened after she had been dressed up as a working girl to get onto the boats – prison hulks. She had really looked the part and I went red every time I thought about her. It was difficult to think straight when she was made up like that.

Her idea meant we needed to do it again. She had moved over to the table and after examining all the stuff on the table she set about doing her face.

'I need to look the part to go out and ask questions,' she said, having picked up a large powdery thing and started dabbing her face.

I was looking around the room to see if there was anything we could use for what I knew of her idea. There was nothing. I tried the windows to see if there was any way we could escape because escaping was always going to be a better idea. We didn't have enough money to pay for this. Those men at the door had looked real trouble. The windows didn't move.

Jen turned around, pulled up her skirt, gave me a twirl and asked me if she looked alright.

To be honest she was scarier than even Miss Tregarthur had managed. Scary in a different way.

'You can shut your mouth now.' Jenna leant over and gave me a kiss. I caught a glance in the mirror over the table. I had a bright red mark across my face. Dad's drug dealers frightened me less.

'Right,' Jen turned serious. 'I'm going to see what I can find out. I'll leave the door open. Any trouble come and save me.'

'W-what,' I stammered.

She laughed again, 'Anyway give a shout, something to get me back in here if it sounds like I'm having trouble. Otherwise I don't know what might happen.' She left.

I wasn't sure what I was meant to shout and I didn't want to picture what the trouble might be. Jenna was the expert here. She left the room and I heard her conversation with the bouncers.

'He's passed out,' she laughed to the men. 'No stamina these country boys.'

I heard the laughs of the two men, along with their own comments of how they thought Jenna could spend her time. That did sound like real trouble but not something I could necessarily do anything about.

'Before I go back and take his money I need to get a message to one of the girls,' Jenna said, after she had turned down their offers.

'Difficult,' one of the men said. 'No idea who we've got in here. We just mind the door. You don't want to talk to Vanderaly about that. She'll throw you out if you're doing anything other than usual business here.'

'That woman's fiercer than the dogs she keeps, bite your arm off, that's how she runs this place,' the other man added.

There were other laughs and noise in the hallway. I heard another girl taking someone into a room further away. A door opened and the sound of music spilled out. The two men were letting people in and out all the time.

'You might know her, new girl, brought in by two men in a carriage. They're waiting over there,' Jenna said, when it became quieter.

'Oh, that one,' the men laughed together.

'They dragged her in,' the first man continued. 'Must have given her something to keep her quiet. Had to carry her up the stairs. She's up there.'

I hoped the man had made it clear where Demelza had been taken.

'Up there with George,' the second man added more: 'He's a regular, not that George is his real name. Not the name his wife calls him by.' And all of them including Jenna laughed at that.

'Best be getting back to check on my country boy first.' I wished Jenna had sounded more convincing, she sounded as though she was losing her courage.

'Stay with us if you like, we're up for anything free.' It sounded as though the men were closing in on her. Time for my shout.

'Where is she?' I called out angrily. 'Get my woman in here.'

And with more laughs Jenna came back into the room.

'About time,' I shouted, hoping I sounded convincing. Jenna was shaking. I held her while she recovered. She might look the part but I could see this had frightened her. Frightened her, terrified me, as did the next part of her idea.

Jenna told me more about her plan. I was to go out.

'It's easier for the paying people, there's some sort of entertaining area. I could see it further down the corridor,' Jenna said, and she was still shaking. 'We know where she is. You can find the one-armed man, offer him money, show them the gold belt, tell him they'll get extra money if they help get Demelza.'

I sat on the bed, probably scratching my head. This was Jenna's idea and I didn't want to rubbish her plan, but it was a crazy idea, couldn't work. The men would see the gold and just take it. If they needed help the two bouncers at the door would probably join in. Anything for a bit of extra money. Even if none of that happened we'd still get stopped. This Vanderaly woman didn't sound as though she'd let us walk out with one of her women – especially if it might mean lost payment. Overall the chance of death was just as high as all the other threats we'd been through – more because there wasn't any sign of rescue.

I had been trying to come up with a better idea while Jenna was flouncing about in the hallway with her two bouncer friends. I guess that's what Jenna had expected. Maybe she thought I needed a bit more pressure – a high chance of dying was quite persuasive.

'Fine,' she said, after hearing my suggestion. 'Let's do it.'

It didn't take too long. This room might not contain any lethal weapons, nothing to blast my way out. But what it did have, as well as the table and bed, were two gas lamps. In fact, for what I might have expected in a brothel the room was quite bright. Maybe it was mostly used by the women to do their makeup. Gas lamps burning bright.

'Fire!' screamed Jenna. 'FIRE, FIRE! He's set the place on fire. HELP!'

Flames and smoke billowed from our room. Fire retardant not yet invented, the feather mattress erupted. We had to get out fast.

Mayhem. At the end of the hall there was a ballroom or bar and it was packed. There had been music and dancing, all part of the brothel. The room emptied out in a frantic rush of people – some scantily dressed and some, well, not actually dressed at all. The building was all wood and it was panic as they rushed for the door. This lot knew the danger of fire in a building with no fire escapes. The management had never been keen on letting people out in a hurry. Now there were trampling, wailing, howling bodies that fought their way out.

No one helped, many fell to the floor. The two bouncers were the first to leave.

'Quick,' Jen pulled me to one side at the bottom of the stairs.

Most of the people had made it downstairs so it wasn't difficult for us to get up. No one was interested in anything we were doing, only interested in escape and staying alive as the flames reached the hallway.

Jenna charged upwards. 'In there,' she shouted, rushing to a door. 'That's where they said she'd be.'

The door was locked but I smashed against it and the wood came apart easily. I supposed that Miss Vanderaly sometimes needed to get into locked rooms.

Inside a man, small and with a look of total confusion – must have been George – sat with his head in his hands. Demelza hadn't made it as far as the bed and was slumped over another chair and snoring.

'She won't wake up,' George moaned, almost as though he hadn't heard the screams of fire.

'We need to get out FAST.' Jenna pointed at the snoring Demelza. 'Get her,' she yelled.

We made for the door.

George followed as if locked in a trance. 'She kept asking for the telly and her phone and would I turn on the central heating,' George said, in a slurred bewildered way. 'Then she just passed out. What's a phone?' George seemed more interested in Demelza's words than escaping with his life. He had hold of Jenna's arm and was demanding answers.

'Tell you when we get out,' Jenna shrugged him off and we went out on to the landing.

Down below the fire had really taken hold. The whole hallway was in flames. There was no way we could escape. The fire had reached the bottom of the stairs, flames and smoke coming up to meet us.

'Back to the room.' I carried Demelza into George's room.

George had done nothing but stare at us with his mouth half open, a hopeless look. His room was larger and more upmarket than the one we'd used downstairs. Probably one for the regular customers. I tried the window but it wouldn't budge, I smashed the glass with a chair and looked out, we were one floor above the ground, only just visible in the dark. Something below glistened in the faint light. This might be the only way out – jumping. Still a long way down, jumping would be dangerous, probably break a leg.

Jenna was shaking George, 'Come on. Is there another way out?'

'No idea,' he said, slowly shaking his head. 'You can call me Herbert if you like, no point in pretending if we are all going to die.'

'That's not going to happen,' Jenna shouted.

Dumping Demelza I rushed out to the smoke filled landing, checking other rooms, they were all the same, bedrooms with no escape route.

'There's no other way out,' I said, returning to the others and sitting on the edge of the bed. 'Wait for the fire brigade?' It wasn't a serious suggestion.

'They won't bother coming here.' George seemed a bit more alive now death was near.

'Sheets,' cried Jenna. 'Tie them together and we can use them as a rope.'

We rushed from room to room dragging off none too clean

sheets from the other beds. Soon we had a pile of them. But tying them together was hopeless, our knots wouldn't hold, the sheets were too coarse, any rope we might end up with was too short.

'No good, should have tried this before we set the place alight,' I said, throwing the sheets to one side. 'Get some of the mattresses off the beds.'

Choking and coughing, we dragged two heavy feather mattresses to George's room. After that thick smoke drove us back. Smoke was starting to come through the floorboards into the room.

'Keep them out of the flames,' Jenna shouted, her voice almost drowned by the sound of the building coming apart. 'The last mattress almost exploded when we set it alight.'

'You did that?' George/Herbert didn't really sound surprised but still did nothing to help.

'I need to smash the rest of the window.' I was finding it hard to see.

'This.' Jenna grabbed at a small wooden chair by the bed and threw it to me.

I crashed the chair into the window, broken glass flying everywhere.

'Quick,' Jenna dragged one mattress and I heaved it out while she pulled the next one towards me and finally the one from George's bed. I hoped I'd made a pile for us to jump onto, I couldn't see enough to be sure.

'Her first,' Jenna pointed to the partially conscious Demelza.

She groaned and tried to struggle when I lifted her but I just pushed her through the window. I heard a screech and a splash and another screech.

'Must be the river,' I shouted. 'Go … go,' as I pushed Jenna out. There was more light from the fire as I saw her hit the mattress pile and bounce into the air sideways. I heard the splash as she hit the water and let out a yell.

George was next. I could have left him, but the flames were through the broken bedroom door, he wouldn't have survived long, so I heaved him out. As he bounced towards the water he was shouting something about not being able to swim. Behind me the fire broke through the floor, the bed disappeared into the furnace below. I leapt.

It wasn't the real river, just a smelly cold backwater, a sewer, didn't need to swim just stand up in the squelchy mud. We waded to the side, away from the building but into a crowd that had gathered to watch. Flames shot high in the sky, the building was a broken shell of blazing timber.

'Good thing,' I heard one woman say. 'Needed clearing out.'

The crowd started to shout and jeer at us. Not sure if it was because they thought we'd been customers or because we stank and dripped with foul smelling mud.

'Get out of here,' a bruised Jenna called while wiping mud from her face and pulling at George's arm.

I threw Demelza over my shoulder. She'd stirred a bit in the water but had gone back to snoring. Whatever the one-armed man had given her it was powerful, something we could have done with on those occasions when an unconscious Demelza would have been helpful.

We pushed through the crowd. They kept away, nobody was likely to stop us – we looked like creatures from a horror movie and smelt like it too. We didn't stop until we were on our own and had reached the edge of the main river – I guess it was the Thames.

Apart from bruises and cuts, we had survived; nothing broken as far as I could tell. Although the water wasn't much cleaner we scraped off the worst of the stinking mess that clung to us. I suggested we chucked Demelza into the water but Jenna was determined to save her, although that was getting a bit over-repetitive. I still gave her a good dunking but she was beyond complaining.

George/Herbert became a different person after we cleaned him up. I guess his dip in the water might have sobered him up. He had sounded rather slurred in the brothel.

'Need a cab,' George said, looking around. 'Get to the road.' We followed him, still carrying Demelza.

Personally if I'd been a cab driver, even a horse drawn one, I would not have stopped for one nearly unconscious and three other dripping stinking passengers. But George stepped into the road and raised his hand. Perhaps cab drivers around here were used to taking people who'd fallen in the river.

I was even more surprised when George said, 'Where to?' and looked at Jenna for directions to tell the driver.

'White Hart, Mile End Road,' Jen called out and we were off.

Was George going to stay with us? It didn't seem a bad idea, he probably lived in London and maybe he could help.

It wasn't long before we made it back. George came into our room; moved into organisation mode. He made them light a fire in our grate, not using the mattress this time. And fixed for us to have a bath, only one. I would have been last but Demelza was still only just awake so she took the last turn, with Jenna cleaning her up and from the yells she didn't do it too gently.

The four of us ended up in our room with George persuading the landlord to find us dry clothes and demanding drinks to be brought up.

'Any chance of a hot chocolate?' asked Jenna. 'With whipped cream and sprinkles,' she added.

George gave her a strange look, 'Sprinkles?'

Jenna said nothing. This was going to get complicated. Herbert kept persuading us to use his real name, I suggested Herbie which he didn't like but which sort of stuck. He didn't show any sign of leaving.

'Haven't you got a home?' Jen asked after we'd drunk his drinks. I wondered who was paying.

'Can't go there tonight, said I'd be away.' Herbie hung his head.

I laughed. Whatever story he had told at home meant he was expected not to go home before the next day. He had obviously been planning to stay at the brothel all night.

'Bit too hot for you to go home?' Jenna actually poked him. He didn't look used to being poked, certainly not by Jenna and he looked embarrassed, maybe not embarrassed enough for Jenna who poked him again. 'Go there a lot do you?'

Herbie changed the subject quickly. 'You said you'd tell me what that girl,' he pointed at Demelza, 'what she meant with those strange words.'

'Why are you so interested?' I asked, strange words were the last thing on my mind after this night of flames and near death.

'I'm a writer,' he said. 'I like new ideas, new things, I write about them.'

'Any good?' Jen sounded cynical.

'People tell me so,' he sniffed. 'Some people say my writing is a bit strange.'

'What name do you use?' Jenna probably thought he was making it all up.

'Wells, Herbert George Wells – HG Wells is the name on my books.'

'Never heard of you,' Jenna and I replied. I didn't think it was likely that we'd know of someone writing a hundred years before our real time at home.

But a slurred voice came from the floor where we'd left snoring Demelza, 'He wrote the time thingy.'

'The what?' came three voices.

'You know, the story about the time machine,' and Demelza slumped back with a noise like a foghorn.

-7-

THE WRITER

We slept that night together in our one room. Herbie seemed to feel he was old enough and important enough to have the bed. Demelza was crashed out and she got the floor. Jenna said she wasn't going to get anywhere near Herbie which meant that I had half the bed.

'Watch him,' Jenna said, before taking a duvet-like thing to lie on. Herbie said it was an eiderdown and with that gone we didn't have much to cover us. 'Cosy up?' Jenna laughed and that made me move nearer to the edge – I certainly didn't want Herbie snuggling up to me in the night.

Jen positioned herself so that Herbie would have to wake her if he had any more ideas about Demelza. Jen's like that – protecting and hating at the same time.

In the early light the street noises were loud enough to wake us.

'I'm hungry,' Demelza wailed, throwing her arms wide. 'Where ....' She stopped and looked around. 'What happened?'

Jenna gave her the full story. I guess she hoped it would shame Herbie but he seemed quite at home about the idea of molesting someone half conscious and probably half his age. He was sitting on the edge of the bed with a smile on his face.

'It's not legal,' Jenna pushed him away.

'She's over thirteen,' Herbie sounded hurt.

'Thirteen?' Jenna raised her voice.

It turned out that thirteen was the age of consent in the 1880s. Demelza gave a smirk and a pout at Herbie who nearly leapt at her before Jenna slapped him down. 'Not a chance, Grandpa.'

'I'm still hungry,' Demelza whined again.

Herbie offered to take us out. 'To one of the coffee houses.'

We left the inn. Herbie stopped. 'Can't go anywhere looking like this.' The clothes the landlord had found us were more usual for us – working smocks, but not for Herbie. We ended up waiting for a shop to open before he went in and bought a complete outfit – waistcoat, jacket, tie, and of course a hat. I asked him if it was expensive.

'Expensive?' Herbie sounded puzzled. 'Oh, I put it on account.'

I thought we should have gone into the shop with him, but probably the three of us looked too dodgy to get credit.

A short walk took us to Warren's House of Coffee. A tall building on the corner of two streets. It looked a bit like an old bank to me. Outside, posters under large arched wooden windows told how their coffee would make us into supermen. Inside the place was busy, smoky and full of noise. Long tables crowded with men, not many women except those running around serving coffee in tall jugs and getting abuse. Everyone shouting to get heard over the noise.

This was to be a place they came to talk about money and business – lots of yelling and arguing about boats and cargo from all over the world. It felt quite modern and the sewers must have been working because it didn't smell so bad.

Herbie was known here. I hoped he was only known for being a writer, not in his 'George' disguise. It meant we had a table to ourselves. Bacon and sausages too.

'So, now you've got to tell me about those strange things you were talking about – phones, sprinkles and things,' Herbie said, when we'd eaten nearly everything they sold.

Before we could answer someone started singing in the street, a hymn, I think. Two people in uniform came charging in, beaming faces as they handed out pamphlets telling us of the dangers of drink.

'Salvation Army.' Herbie told them to push off which started an argument made worse by Jenna suggesting Herbie was an ideal person to go to one of their meetings.

Herbie returned to his questions.

Demelza stepped in: 'We're from the future, well, actually, you're from the past,' she jumped as Jenna gave her a kick.

'Why shouldn't I tell him that?' Demelza sounded cross. 'Herbie writes about time travel so it shouldn't be a problem.'

'Look,' Herbie had a sharp tone to his voice and appeared recovered from the near death fire last night. 'Look if you aren't going to use a proper name could you at least call me HG.'

'HG it is,' said Jenna.

The previous night had left us all more than a bit strange. Near death experiences might be getting a bit common for us but that didn't mean we weren't shaken. I still hadn't worked out why Demelza had been kidnapped or who had done the kidnapping.

Jenna and I were sitting at the end of the table and started talking as quietly as we could, difficult in this place. 'She must have done it,' Jenna suggested that Miss Tregarthur must have been involved.

'How did she even know we were here?' I said.

'Maybe when you asked questions about Masterson, when you went to the city,' Jenna said, as another pot of coffee landed in front of us. Herbie took it and was going to pinch the waitress before Jen smacked his hand away.

Jenna's suggestion seemed possible, there were a lot of people on the streets and someone rich like Masterson could easily get information, probably people selling it to him. Jenna and I carried on talking and forgot about Demelza who had moved in on Herbie and was telling him all about our time travelling. Not really a great idea.

Herbie jumped to his feet, slammed the table. 'You've been sent to make a fool of me, haven't you?' he cried out. 'That's what you're doing, isn't it?' He turned to each of us, looking for confirmation. 'Who paid you? What ….' He trailed off and sat down again. That might have caused a problem in Costa but there was so much shouting in here that no one noticed.

'OK, I … err … it's...' I was trying to come up with some sort of explanation.

'Okay? What's that mean?' HG butted in.

'We need help,' Jenna shifted the conversation. 'There's this mad woman and she's up to something. We need to find out what it is, so we can get back home.'

'To the future,' HG laughed.

Jenna looked at me, I wasn't sure what she wanted.

'Or at least to Dartmoor.' I hoped that this would be a simpler problem for HG to deal with.

'Why should I help?' It was obvious that HG felt we were a load of hoaxers and probably after his money.

'We could tell your family about George.' I might not be after his money but a bit of blackmail seemed reasonable.

'Don't think they'd care, it's not a crime,' HG smiled. 'You'll have to try harder than that.'

'How about an idea for a new book?' Demelza had finished three cups of chocolate and some of her old self had returned. That wasn't all good. I didn't remember anything positive about her when we'd been at school.

'I've got ideas,' Herbie said, in a dreamy and uncertain voice.

'Like what?' Demelza was good at picking up on uncertainty.

'Like …'

'Like writing about a time machine to take you into the future?'

'Maybe,' Herbie looked at her. 'How do you know that?'

'Come on Herbie, help us and we'll tell you how to write a real best-seller.' Demelza gave him a smile which was definitely over the age of consent and we watched the man melt. Demelza might not be a good person but she might be useful. Not sure that was an idea I wanted to share with Jenna.

'Ummm … I'm already...' HG stopped and looked a bit shocked but it looked like he was interested.

Demelza turned to me and whispered, 'I saw the film.'

'Film? Is that another future thing?' HG had heard her words.

'I'll tell you all about it after you've helped us.' Demelza was good at manipulation. Even Jenna looked impressed. I had a nasty feeling that HG was going to want more than a story from Demelza but we'd have to deal with that later.

'What sort of help?' he asked looking at Demelza but she passed over to Jen to explain.

'It's about this man Masterson …' Jenna started.

'Masterson,' HG interrupted. 'Everyone's talking about him.' He waved his hand around the room. 'Everyone.'

I thought I had heard his name mentioned by a group when we first came in here.

'He's buying all sorts of things,' HG sounded envious.

'Including that park.' I wondered what he knew.

'Doubt he'll get that,' HG said. 'There will be a great deal of opposition, but he is definitely after some of the land up there. Don't know why, it's a swamp. But what do you want with him?' HG looked at us as though it was improbable that three strange, young and probably penniless people could have anything sensible to do with the rich and powerful.

'That's because of … the woman I was talking about,' Jenna said, and I thought she was right not to give away too much.

'There's talk about a strange looking wild woman going around with him. Some people are saying he's taken up with witchcraft,' HG said.

'Miss Tregarthur's more than a witch,' Demelza chipped in not caring about what she said. 'We've got to get the crystal back from … Ow!' She shrieked at the kick from Jenna. But it didn't stop her. 'No point in not telling him the whole story and don't kick me again. HG here won't do anything to help unless I ask him. Will you Herbie?'

I didn't like to imagine what was going on in HG's mind, but Demelza did have a point. Winding people around her finger was one of her best skills. A skill that had almost killed us.

I could see Jenna really wasn't happy. 'We don't have to go into all the detail.' Jenna looked ready to kick again. 'But it's true. We need to get this crystal so that we can go home.'

'Crystals, the moor and the future?' HG sneered.

'Yes,' all three of us said at the same time.

'And she won't give it to you easily, I expect?' HG could already see problems even if he didn't believe us. 'Have you asked her?'

All sorts of ideas of what I'd like to do to Miss Tregarthur had sat in my mind since the death of my mother, *asking* her anything came low down on the list. 'You'd have to do more than ask,' I said.

'Masterson has a house not far from here,' HG went on. 'Why don't I just go round there and see what's happening?'

'You could do that?' It didn't sound possible to me. I was remembering the men guarding his other houses.

I suppose we were lucky that he was a writer and fiction was something he knew. Jumping out of burning buildings and talk of time travel could well feature in one of his books.

'Being a writer has certain … advantages … people do things for you.' He looked at Demelza.

'Stop looking at her like that you perv,' Jenna said loudly and gave HG one of her pokes which got another 'Ow' and I suspected a kick might have been sent under the table but must have missed because Demelza followed HG's earlier sneer with a smirk of her own.

'You can just turn up at his house and ask him?'

'Absolutely.' I thought I heard a tiny touch of anxiety in HG's voice. 'You stay here and I'll come back and tell you what he says. You just have to tell me a bit more.'

I didn't know what to say. I looked at Jenna and she didn't say anything.

'Um,' was all I managed.

'Just tell him,' Demelza raised her voice. 'Tell Herbie all about her or he won't know what to ask.'

With neither of us speaking Demelza went on: 'Miss Tregarthur is weird …'

'Weird?' HG interrupted her. 'She controls destiny?'

'Eh?' Demelza was thrown by the question. 'I suppose she does, in a way.'

It seemed that the word "weird" had a different meaning in those days.

'Anyway she's weird,' Demelza started again. I wasn't sure if Jenna felt this was any sort of good idea – letting Demelza babble on. I waited to see what she said. We might learn something.

'She took us on this walk,' Demelza did her babbling on. 'Then there was this earthquake and we ended up in this weird place.'

'Weird place? Weird person, weird place. Interesting use of words.' HG pulled a notebook and pencil out of his new coat pocket and scribbled in it, I suppose words were really important to him as a writer. I think he was more interested in the words than in listening to Demelza. Possibly he believed he should be the expert and not us. I wondered how he'd got the notebook.

Demelza was still going on and I'd forgotten just how annoying she really was; her voice was more of a whine than a babble. 'Weird, strange, odd, bizarre,' Demelza puffed. 'And stop interrupting, Herbie.'

'Anyway Alvin here tried to take charge and …' Demelza stopped.

'Ah, yes, Demelza,' Jenna said. 'Why don't you tell us all what happened?'

Demelza went into a sulky silence.

'Miss Tregarthur – the weird one,' Jenna took over. 'She's …'

'The one from the future,' HG laughed.

'Stop interrupting!' the three of us said together.

'Yes, she's from your future, not ours, she's from our time.' Jenna's words stopped HG. 'She has been wandering through time, mostly trying to get us killed. I mean me and Alvin, not Demelza, she has been helping her.'

Demelza's mouth opened and closed, she had nothing to say.

Jenna went on: "This time I didn't think she knew we were here, although ...' Jenna shot me a look. 'Whatever she's doing it won't be good. She's up to something with this Masterson man. We need to find out more and we need to stop her.'

'We have to get the crystal,' Demelza chipped in. I could see she wanted to make herself more important, but was that a good idea? Telling HG about the crystal? Well, she'd done it now.

'You don't need to ask Masterson about the crystal,' Jenna snapped. 'She won't have told him about that.'

'Why not?' Demelza whined.

'Need to find out what other weird things Masterson is doing at Hampstead, what other plans he has.' I wanted to get him away from talking about the crystal and I threw in another 'weird' as bait. We had no idea if we could trust him. If he got hold of the crystal he might not give it to us, he might have other ideas, *I* would. It had to be valuable even if it wasn't any use.

'How many meanings has this word?' HG took the bait.

Jenna went on to give him a bit more information, leaving out other places and times we'd been to. 'We have to find her,' she finished.

'To get the crystal?' HG hadn't been entirely diverted.

We all nodded.

'I see you don't want to tell me everything,' HG almost smiled. 'Doesn't matter. I'll go and see him, I want to find out more weird things. You can stay here until I return.'

-8-

A Visit

Although it would have been possible to stay in this coffee house for as long as we wanted, Jenna decided we should go with him. At least we would know where Masterson lived. HG put the bill on another tab or whatever they called it, didn't seem any likelihood of it being paid to me but apparently the owner liked to tell everyone that the famous writer drank coffee here.

We set off on foot. HG knew the streets and only had to ask directions a couple of times. HG was whistling as we walked, not a wonderful sound. I think it was about confidence, he wanted us to believe he could carry this off but wasn't so sure himself.

We arrived at an impressive building in a broad street. It looked more like the sort of building that should have been a library. Probably would become one in our time, a library or town hall, big enough. We waited across the street. HG rang the bell and they let him in. No questions asked, no one bringing out guns or telling him to clear off. We waited and waited.

'Must be going alright,' Jenna shuffled her feet on the pavement. 'He's been in there for ages.'

Not long after she said that the front door flew open and it didn't seem to be going well at all.

'Leave me alone. LEAVE ME ALONE.'

HG left the house to the sound of shouts from inside. 'Don't do it, you stupid man,' HG shouted back.

Two other men appeared. They had to be servants because they were wearing uniforms similar to the ones that the guards had been wearing at his other two houses – how many houses did he need? The servants definitely didn't look friendly.

HG left at a quick walk, looking back over his shoulder as he joined us. 'Quick, we need to get away from here, get away from that crazy, stupid, man. He'll kill us all.'

As we hurried off HG kept repeating: 'He's crazy, awful terrible notions he has, so dangerous.'

'What did he tell you?' Jen sounded frantic. 'Did you find out anything?'

'Terrible things,' HG muttered and carried on walking quickly.

I stopped him, 'What about Miss Tregarthur?'

HG tried to push past me, 'We have to get away.' Again he looked back at Masterson's house. 'But we have to get that thing away from him, must take the book, must stop him. Have to make a plan.'

He tried to push against me. I didn't budge. 'Miss Tregarthur? We don't move until you tell me.'

'Who? What?' HG seemed to have forgotten. 'Oh her. He said she'd gone.'

'Gone where?' I shouted.

'Gone … well … gone,' HG muttered.

'Where?' I grabbed his jacket and shook him.

'Into her time machine, that's what the crazy man said, into her time machine, you're all barking mad, there's no such thing.' HG paused. 'Is there?'

I guess it felt like everything stopped, as though the three of us and HG were standing in a separate silent bubble, not hearing the horses, the shouting, any of the noise going on around us. No idea how long that lasted.

HG broke in eventually, 'Is there? No such thing.'

'That's it,' Jenna said, staring at a pile of horse dung in the road. 'We're stuck here forever. No way home even if we had got the crystal to work again. She's gone, must have gone into the tunnel, found a way to make it work for her again.'

'What are you going to do?' Demelza said into Jenna's face. 'Eh? What?'

I could see Jenna was about to blow and I didn't care. Instead Jenna found a use for the horse dung and with a shove Demelza sprawled into the steaming pile and started howling. We walked away.

HG stayed and pulled her out, gave her a handkerchief and shouted after us, 'She's coming back, if you can believe it, coming back through time.'

'What?' I turned on him. 'Why didn't you say that before?'

I didn't get too close, you could smell Demelza from a distance and as she wiped off the horse dung with HG's handkerchief, I could see she was thinking about throwing bits in our direction.

'Crazy story, time travel indeed.' HG had also taken a few steps away.

'What did Masterson say about her coming back?' I asked.

'Your weird woman has Masterson in a dreadful state. She really frightened him.' HG shook his head although I think he liked using the word "weird". 'He made no sense. He said she was coming to make sure he'd done what she told him.'

HG wouldn't say any more until we arrived back at the coffee house and he had bought a change of smock dress for Demelza. We had a different table on the first floor.

Downstairs a rowdy mass of people were jostling and shouting. I heard more mention of Masterson's name along with shouts to buy all sorts of things: tea, coffee, wool and some mention of iron works. And, of course, politics, which flew right over my head.

Jenna is everything to me but she isn't what you'd call a natural beauty like Demelza who was swishing herself through the throng of people and enjoying the looks and calls before we found our table. The new dress helped.

'I could almost believe you, after speaking to him.' HG had plonked himself down in a chair.

'Not as easy as you thought, getting to talk to him?' Jen was scowling at Demelza.

'Oh that was easy enough, to get in there and ask him questions. Most of the conversation went well. When we turned to politics it became a little sticky, and when he started spouting on about war machines, I really couldn't listen to him without telling him the truth.'

'Which is?' I asked.

'War never works, we need peace,' HG said, as though it was obvious. 'Making new war machines will make it worse.'

I wasn't going to disagree with him, but I couldn't see why we'd got on to war. 'What did he say about Miss Tregarthur?'

'We need to know or you won't get that story,' Demelza slurred, she had stopped flirting and was slumped in her chair and yawning. I suppose it was the hangover, from whatever they'd given her yesterday, that had caught up with her.

HG gave her an odd look, not like the slobbering ones before. 'Masterson said we'd all get the same treatment as Demelza.'

'What?' Was it me or Jenna who shouted?

'He knew what happened to Demelza?' I said, slowly. 'Thought he might.'

'Wasn't my fault,' HG said, as though we were accusing him of abduction as well as everything else. 'I had no idea she was going to be unconscious.'

I leant across the table and grabbed his arm. 'What did she do?'

'She?' HG squirmed, my grip was stronger and more painful than I meant.

I let go. 'Miss Tregarthur. What did she do to him?'

HG rubbed his arm. 'She knows all about you, arranged for Demelza to get kidnapped, thought you'd all follow. She had planned to kill you all, so you've got me to thank for getting you out of that place.'

I didn't feel HG deserved any thanks for anything that had happened at the brothel. But maybe he was right, it wasn't only the fire we had escaped. I did wonder why the men who kidnapped Demelza had gone back to the place. Surely they had done what they had been asked and delivered her to the brothel. Perhaps they had gone back to wait for us. They probably knew we were watching the Captain Kidd, knew we would follow them. We must have just escaped when Jenna was so quick to push us into that room.

'Why did she want me dead?' slurred Demelza. 'Haven't I done everything she asked?' And she almost sobbed.

If she hadn't been in that semi-conscious state, Jenna would have found some more horse dung. But Demelza had a point. Why did Miss Tregarthur want to kill her? I knew she was determined to do away with me, but why Demelza?

Jenna must have been thinking the same and whispered to me, 'That must be because she knows something that we don't.'

'How would she know Demelza hasn't told us already?' I whispered.

'I guess that if we knew what it was, then we could be doing something else that actually worked. There must be another way, something we don't know yet that means Miss Tregarthur can use the time tunnel again.' Jenna looked at the snoring Demelza. 'We have to get it out of her, but later.'

A group of men in the coffee house came and spoke to HG. One of them, a man with a huge beer belly, wanted to know if he could be included in his next book. HG said he'd try and they left.

'What he doesn't know is that he's already been in one of my stories – he wouldn't like the character I wrote about,' HG laughed. 'A bit too close to how he is in real life.'

HG was dreaming about writing and it was difficult to hold him to our questions.

Jenna slapped her hand on the table, 'Did Masterson know why she left?'

'Masterson showed me her book,' HG didn't sound as though he wanted to talk about it. 'He said it was the most important book in history, but the way he held it showed me he was terribly frightened.'

'What book?' I said.

'Told you she had a book.' Demelza knocked over a mug of coffee.

'A book of terrible ideas,' HG answered after we'd cleared up the mess. 'Actually it was only a portion of the book, ripped out pages held together by the cover, your woman must have kept the rest.'

I shot a puzzled look at Jenna.

Demelza slipped from her seat on to the floor, bashed her head and grunted, 'OW.' Before sitting up, rubbing herself and saying, 'Told you she had a book, told her what was going on, like an encyclopaedia.'

'It had pictures of awful machines,' HG said. 'Things that never should be made, and it told him how to make them.'

'Machines?' I frowned.

'Machines of war. Huge guns and rockets and something called tanks and … and … submarines,' HG said.

We had to stop again as another group of men came over to HG and started talking about writing and stories. We waited, wondering what Miss Tregarthur had been doing. It just couldn't be good. Eventually the men left. I think they had been disappointed. HG had said so little. He was a man in shock. Whatever had been in this book had not just frightened Masterson. Part of me didn't want to find out.

'She said he had to build them,' HG said after they had gone. 'Had to.' His face creased; were those tears in his eyes? 'It's the war. She told him that there was going to be a war of the whole world. Terrible.' HG leant forward with his head in his hands. 'Don't ask me anymore, please.'

It took us more hot chocolate and long pauses to get the whole story. And it was a crazy story, the sort we'd come to expect from Miss Tregarthur.

'I get it now,' Jenna said. 'This book was written in our time, so having it in this time means it tells of the future. These war things haven't been invented yet.'

'And I won't let them ever be invented.' HG sat up again. 'We must get the book, we must.'

'Is it just the money? Remember that crazy idea she had before, with her brother or whoever he was, making gas pipes or whatever?' I said.

'Surely there's more than money, let's go,' Jenna stood up.

We walked back to the inn. HG had left us and perhaps we should have asked him more questions, but the thought of being here forever was stuck in our minds.

Demelza demanded another bath and after that was more awake and wanted to join in trying to make sense of what HG had told us. 'Miss Tregarthur wants to make all these guns and rockets and things and sell them when the war starts.'

'This can't be just money,' Jenna frowned. 'Can it?'

'It'll be the First World War,' Demelza said, as though that was obvious.

'Do we care?' It wasn't obvious to me.

'HG said there was something even worse in the book,' Jenna's voice cracked. 'Much worse, a big cloud, a mushroom cloud, that book has details of how to make a nuclear bomb.'

That took a few minutes to sink in. A nuclear bomb in the First World War? Even I knew about that war. A war with horses and mud and trenches and so many deaths, millions. What would happen if a nuclear bomb was used in that war?

'Bad enough in the second world war,' Jenna said.

'But if they had a nuclear bomb, couldn't they have stopped the war happening?' Wasn't that a good idea? The trouble was I didn't believe there was anything ever good about Miss Tregarthur's ideas.

'What, nuke Germany?' Jenna said, as though it was obviously a stupid idea. 'She won't stop there. Imagine Miss Tregarthur with a nuclear bomb. And there's something worse.'

Jenna was interrupted by a loud knock at our door, HG barged in. 'We've got to stop him. We must stop him.' HG dropped a heavy bag on to the bed. It fell open. Iron bars and other tools. The sort of things you might imagine could be used for breaking into houses. 'We have to get that book.' He picked up one of the bars and smacked it into the palm of his hand. 'We must destroy it.'

I wasn't sure if getting the book was our problem. The tunnel was more important. If we made it back to our own time, then … but … wait … if Miss Tregarthur started using nuclear bombs in the First World War what would happen to our future? Would the future change if she changed the past?

I was still surprised when Jenna said, 'He's right, we have to get the book. What has HG brought in his bag, Alvin?' She looked at me, as the expert.

I emptied the bag and picked over the contents. Reluctantly, well probably reluctantly, I shared the things I had overheard at home. Of course I'd never been involved in house breaking, too young for my dad and my brother to use me for that – even though they'd wondered if I could slip through windows – but Mum had stopped that while she was still around.

HG was a bit deflated when I told him his bag of tools were probably useless. He had wanted to break the door open at night, creep in and take the book. It was probably the sort of thing that happened in his books.

'He'll always have people there. Those men in uniform. You'll never get past them,' Jenna said.

'Suppose so but …' HG was still trying to talk up his plan. 'We can use these,' and he produced a sock filled with sand. 'Hit them over the head.' HG smashed the sock down on the side of the bed. 'Like this.'

The sight was ridiculous, but at least it made us laugh.

'Distraction,' I explained. 'What we need is a big distraction.'

It took several days of planning. We were all taken up by planning our great house breaking adventure. I could see that HG was lost in a sort of fantasy world, as though he was writing about house breaking rather than actually planning to do it.

'You could go out and keep track of Masterson,' Jenna suggested, to give him something safer to do because he kept suggesting we got hold of a few guns, which would have been a seriously bad idea.

HG must have realised why Jenna made the suggestion but he still did it and came back to us with news: 'Masterson's asking all sorts of merchants how to get hold of things they have never heard of. They say he's gone crazy, needs help.'

I guess asking around in East London for nuclear bomb making materials would be crazy.

'Don't believe they've even discovered radiation in this time,' Jenna said.

Radiation? That made me think. Made me think there was more going on. Did radiation have something to do with the crystal? I decided to keep that thought to myself for the time being, there were too many other details to work out – like house breaking and the distraction.

-9-

The Riot

It was easier than I thought to organise a distraction in that time in history, providing you had enough money. HG was so driven to stop Masterson and get the book of horrors, as he called it, so driven that he would have spent everything he had. But, as it turned out, there were people prepared to have a fight and the money was just an added bonus to them.

All I had to do was go out into the streets of East London and ask. I mean we, because Jenna came as well. We went down to the river, a place of dirt and smells and men standing around with no work, no food and no plans. They didn't believe us at first.

'We need broken glass, shouting, horses going berserk, a cart pushed over, set alight,' Jenna said to a group of men who looked both dangerous and desperate.

'And you'll pay us for that?' One man asked as though it was something they did all the time for free.

We nodded, keeping an eye out for a quick escape in case they decided to practise on us.

'Fine,' they said. We fixed a price.

'More if you want us to kill someone,' one said seriously.

'No need,' I said quickly.

They wanted all the money up front. I gave them just enough

to make it happen, promising the rest on results. I made sure they knew I didn't have all the money with me at the time – they might like the idea of a street battle but taking the money from me without having to do anything would have been just as good an option.

I offered to find more people, another group to make sure a fight actually happened but they laughed and said they knew lots of people who they wanted to have a go at.

'Not a problem, at all,' the one who suggested murder said with a smile. We had the makings of our distraction. They had a riot in mind.

Demelza did nothing to help. Jenna tried to get her involved but she just huffed and walked away. She was doing a lot of walking away, out on the street. When we did meet up she was more interested in telling us what she had seen.

'It's a whole circus out there,' she said, cutting into our planning meeting. 'You should see it, men with animals doing tricks, women selling food – like eels. Can you imagine it?'

'If you aren't going to help, just shut it,' Jenna turned on her.

Not having her involved made planning easier, and I certainly thought she wouldn't be any use in a street fight. So we let her spend the time wandering around and bringing back her tales. We had too much to worry about without worrying about Demelza. I should have realised that was a mistake.

HG insisted that he came with me on the break-in because he knew the layout of the building. He said Masterson would keep the book in his library. I could see that having him with me would be a disaster. I had no idea how HG would behave, probably get into an argument about words rather than trying to escape.

'Everybody knows you,' Demelza said. 'Whatever happens anyone can just come and find you afterwards, even if it works out.'

'But …' HG said, but I could see his mind working, Demelza was right, he'd give us all away. I wondered what had made Demelza suggest it.

HG agreed in the end and moved on to giving me details about the house. The way he gave me those details made it very clear that he was not a man to take on a burglary.

'There's a great hallway, with a marble floor and statues of great men all around. There was Plato, Aristotle and …' HG started a lecture.

'And the book?' I interrupted him.

'Oh, but …' HG wanted to tell me about the statues of great men.

'The book,' I said. 'Where will he have the book?'

'That will be in his library, of course.' HG gave me the sort of look some of my teachers had given me when something was obvious to them and not to me.

I didn't want to take HG with me but this was confusing. I was certainly baffled that a man should have his own library at all. I waited for him to go on.

'There are five or six doors leading from the hallway, I think,' HG said. 'Just make for the one on the left hand.' He stopped. 'No, it's the one in the middle, that's his library.'

'Are you sure? The door in the middle at the back of the hallway?' I groaned.

'Certain,' HG almost grinned. 'Now I remember. The door has an inscription above it, a quote from Goethe, "Talent develops in quiet places" or rather "Es bildet ein talent …'

'Right,' I stopped him giving me another lecture because none of what he was saying made sense or helped. 'Definitely the door in the middle at the back? Below the goat?'

'Goethe, the writer,' HG gave the sniff of someone feeling very superior to me. Fine, at least I wouldn't have him going on about this Goat man while we tried to break in.

We waited for dark.

The street around Masterson's house was wide and usually quiet. The buildings were all large and expensive. It looked like a row of town halls to me. With all those posh people I worried that the police would arrive as soon as we started our riot. But we only wanted a few minutes of distraction and the men said they'd be away before any police could get there.

I went with Jenna, leaving HG and Demelza at the inn. I had to hope they would stay there. If HG was seen, we were in trouble. If Demelza was there we'd be in trouble anyway.

The men said they would wait at the end of the street for my signal. The plan was that I would hurl a beer bottle into the air and when it smashed our hired thugs would set about causing the distraction. They didn't wait.

As soon as they saw me on the street they charged out from all over the place. I think that many of the men thought this was a good time to settle arguments. There must have been nearly a hundred people: yelling, fighting, setting light to several carts, along with people who had come to watch. HG had his money's worth. I wondered how anyone was ever going to get it to stop.

It wasn't long before all the residents came out of their houses to watch. Everyone came out. Masterson's front door opened and his servants poured out – cheering at the fight. The door stayed open.

Jenna waited for me while I slipped inside, without any trouble, absolutely no trouble at all, so easy.

The hallway was amazing and would have been worth a lecture from HG if he had actually remembered the correct details. You could have parked a bus in it, even a horse drawn one. This was nothing like the place HG had described. There was no door in the middle, lots of other doors, none in the middle. A huge staircase curved upwards on one side. On the other a fire burnt in a marble fireplace. There were several doors. Around me, HG's statues almost danced in the flickering light. Electricity had not yet been installed here. I went for a door on the left hoping HG's first memory had been better than the rest. It was.

The library was easy to recognise. Books lined every wall in this gloomy room.

In the fireplace another fire burned brightly, more brightly than the gas lamps. Several leather armchairs with high backs stood in front of the fire. The room was dark and quiet, until …

'She said you would come, a silly girl but she was right,' came a voice from one of the armchairs and a man stood up to face me.

I stopped and groaned. This had to be Masterson, older that I'd thought, balding, a bit overweight, but very much at home and looking very calm.

'I've always had enough people on the streets anyway, to

hear what you planned for tonight. You're after that,' and he pointed to a few battered pages from a book, laid out on a table in front of him. 'You can't stop me. I have to do this, otherwise ...'

I turned for the door. Another man stood in my way.

'She told me what happens in the War, what will happen to my family, it's all there in those pages, all about the war. She said my family will all get killed, my sons dying in the mud somewhere, never to be seen again. I have to stop that. These machines of war and this bomb will stop that happening.'

Masterson seemed determined to tell me more. I barely listened as I tried to work out if I could escape. The door opened and five or six of his uniformed men stood outside. Between them they held Jenna who screamed and shouted and struggled but it was no use.

'It's over,' Masterson said, almost as if he hoped we would put up more of our own fight. His army of servants certainly looked up for it.

'Destroying a whole country is worth it?' Jenna had given up struggling.

'Has to be done,' he sighed, almost as though he wanted us to believe he would regret destroying millions of lives. I didn't believe that he would have any regrets at all. This man had money and power. With the added power of a nuclear bomb so long before anyone else, it would be a disaster. We had to stop him. I grabbed the book. Blank pages fell from my hand.

'You think I'm stupid?' Masterson said, as though it was me he felt was the stupid one. 'That's not it, not the real thing, of course, that's in my safe.'

Marble halls, a library and a safe. I was out of my depth here, it was over. I had no idea what would happen to us. But what was it Masterson had said? 'Silly girl'.

I turned to him, 'Who said we would come?'

'Just a girl,' he answered.

'Demelza,' I said to Jenna.

'That was her name,' Masterson confirmed my fears. He looked so confident, so pleased with himself.

Demelza had sold us out. Where was she now? Her and HG, they must have another plan? That was why she persuaded him not to come.

Masterson pointed to the door and we were taken back into the hallway. We hadn't destroyed the book. We were caught. All our planning was useless. My dad would have had a better plan. I wasn't good at this. I didn't really want to be good at it.

'You can come out now,' Masterson, full of confidence, clapped his hands and called. Other doors opened and two small children ran out with a woman who might have been their mother or more likely another servant from her dress.

The smallest ran to Masterson and jumped into his arms as she shouted, 'Daddy, Daddy.'

'It's alright now, my little ones,' he smiled at the children. 'Daddy has caught all the bad people, all safe now. You can see them over there.' He pointed at us and gave the little girl a kiss on the forehead.

Through the open front door, the noise on the street was even louder. It sounded as though a war had started. Stopping that wasn't going to be my problem anymore. We had to get away, but surely that was impossible.

Impossible became far worse. Noises outside grew even louder with people screaming. The front door crashed wide open on its hinges. With a thunderous roar a huge brown shape charged into the hallway. Giving another roar the beast reared up on its hind legs, a brown monster, taller than any of the statues. A roaring, snarling bear with razor sharp claws searching out its victims.

The children screamed, Masterson screamed. The bear went straight for them.

'No,' Masterson cowered, dropping his daughter and seeming to push her forward as he hid behind one of his marble statues.

The animal towered above the tiny frozen child. She covered her eyes as the bear roared again, raising its vicious claws to strike.

We'd done bears. We'd even eaten a bear back in time. It had kept us alive. That didn't make me less scared now. A bear, here in London, how, where? Demelza had said the streets were like a circus with animals … yes, Demelza had said that, Demelza again.

The hallway emptied. Masterson's servants flew out of the front door. Jenna and I were free, all we had to do was run.

Jenna prodded me hard, handed me a poker from the fire with another in her hand, screaming: 'GO, GO,' and pushed me forward as we ran at the beast. My mind flashed up that this had to be the worst of Jenna's bad ideas.

Jenna got to the animal first, lunging with her poker. I followed, expecting the bear to lunge back. Jenna struck first with her red hot poker. The bear gave a howling yell. A smell of burning fur. It was only a glancing injury for such a huge beast, making it even angrier. I flashed a glance at Jenna hoping it told her how much I felt for her in our last moments.

We jumped backwards as the bear fell towards us. Another growl, we could smell its breath, see the teeth, the claws coming to tear us apart. Our backs against the wall, no chance to escape its flailing arms.

It didn't happen.

Peering out through half closed eyes I saw the animal twitch, its head turned, as though it heard a new sound, sniffed the air, turned again and lumbered out into the street.

Back outside, the screams and shouts quickly grew louder as the bear went through the door along with a stampede of people running. A whistle sounded out, I thought that would be the police. But had it been another call to the bear?

Masterson, emerging from the shadow of his statue, ran to the front door, slammed it shut, throwing bolts across at the top and bottom, turning and sliding down to sit on the floor.

The hall was in chaos. Statues lay toppled and broken, pushed by fleeing servants. A table with flowers was overturned and water was pouring from a broken vase onto the marble floor. Jenna, of course, had one arm holding the small trembling girl and her other around the slightly older boy. We were the only ones left.

'The book,' I said, standing over Masterson.

He just buried his head in his hands.

'The book,' I repeated, and pulled him to his feet.

'Never,' Masterson whimpered. 'Get out, leave me alone.'

'The book, or we tell everyone out there what happened. How you pushed your child towards the bear to save yourself and let her die.' I saw the fear in his eyes. A man for whom reputation would be so important.

'And it would be easy for that fire to get out of control,'

Jenna nodded at the fireplace while still holding the children.

'My men will soon stop you,' Masterson's voice wavered, we were the only ones in the hall. I still had the poker in my hand and the door was bolted shut.

'The book,' Jenna and I said.

'Daddy, just give it to them,' the small girl said to her father. 'GIVE IT NOW.'

-10-

It Isn't Curry

The street was quiet when we left Masterson's house. The bear must have stopped the riot when it ran out into the street. The rioters hadn't stayed, not even for the rest of their money, although they had left an old lady to wait around the corner who stopped us with her stick.

'Brave of them to stay,' Jenna handed over the cash and the lady grunted at her before waddling away without a word.

Further on, we saw the bear again, held on a chain by a man with a whip. The animal was quieter, sitting on the ground, almost asleep. This looked like a circus animal, one like Demelza had said she had seen. Demelza again. Jenna wanted to ask the man questions.

'Need to get back to the inn.' I pulled her away and started to run.

We were only just in time. Demelza and HG were at the door and about to leave.

'Alvin,' Demelza stared. 'I didn't expect ...'

'Didn't expect us to be alive?' Jenna moved forward and pinned Demelza to the wall. HG looked as though he might intervene but I shook my head.

'You told him, you told him we were coming.' Jenna thumped Demelza into the wall.

'I didn't … never … don't,' Demelza whined and I saw her head thump backwards.

'Why did you side with her?' I turned on HG. 'Why?'

'She told me all the things you'd done to her, the things you would do, how you'd tried to kill her, she wasn't safe, I needed to get her away,' HG's mouth was flapping with his words. I could see he recognised the lies.

'I can guess what was in your mind,' Jenna almost spat at him. 'And yours too.' Demelza's head hit the wall again.

'Who was the bear meant to kill? Was that just insurance in case Masterson didn't finish us off?' I hadn't been certain that the animal had been her idea, but the wide-eyed look she gave me confirmed that it was and that was rewarded by another crash as her head hit the wall. Slowly Demelza slid downwards, Jenna let her fall to the floor, before sitting on her.

Jenna let out a loud 'ouch', feeling behind her into Demelza's jacket which she had sat on.

'What?' Jenna held up a small stone.

It wasn't a stone. Sparkling in the light I could see this was a piece of the crystal, a piece of the one Miss Tregarthur had held, had used to control the time tunnel. Jenna's hands were at Demelza's throat, squeezing.

'It's not, it's not,' Demelza gurgled.

'Not what?' Jenna eased off a little.

'Not what you think.' Demelza tried to sit up, Jenna pushed her down.

'What is it then?' I joined in as I held back HG who kept telling us to stop hurting her.

'Let me up and I'll tell you.'

Jenna pulled her to sitting and banged her head once more.

'One lie and I smash a hole in the wall with your head.'

'That piece came off,' Demelza squeaked. 'When she hit the whole crystal.'

With a lot more head banging, we got more of the story. Miss Tregarthur, when trying to get the tunnel to work, had hit her crystal over and over again, a small fragment had broken off. Demelza had managed to grab and hide it before Zach was shot.

Demelza tried to make out that the bear was part of the distraction in the street. 'I thought I was helping,' she said, obviously lying.

'It was me, I found the man with the bear,' HG confessed. 'She said she wanted it to be a secret.'

'How did he control the animal?' I asked.

'He's taught it to respond to the whistle,' HG explained. 'It's the chain with the ring in its nose, it hurts. He used to blow the whistle and pull the chain, now he just has to blow the whistle. The bear's scared.'

Demelza was trying to crawl away.

'Can we do that with her?' Jenna pulled her back. 'The ring through the nose?'

'The man said the bear was quite gentle. Wouldn't harm anyone,' Demelza said in a voice that screamed a lie.

'That's not what …' HG started.

Demelza tried to tell him to shut up, he wouldn't and told us that the bear handler was planning to get rid of the bear because it was too dangerous. 'Kept trying to attack people.'

'And eat small children?' I explained to HG what had happened. Demelza did not look surprised.

'You wanted us all to die?' Jenna shoved her head again and getting no answer started smacking Demelza around the face.

At first Demelza kept denying it, saying she was trying to help.

'I didn't need you,' Demelza sobbed. 'I had the piece of crystal. I don't need you.'

Jenna stopped. 'But if Miss Tregarthur couldn't get the crystal to call the tunnel, what good would your piece be?'

'That may be my fault,' HG butted in. 'Let her up, we'll get a drink and I'll explain. I thought the man would stop the bear. The plan wasn't to kill you.'

'Perhaps not your plan. I'm sure it was Demelza's,' Jenna snarled at her. 'And stop snivelling, we all know it's put on. I can't wait to hear more of your lies.'

We moved into the bar with its low beams and another fire smouldering in the grate. There weren't many people staying at this inn but all of them must have been listening to us. It wouldn't be long before they connected us to the riot we had organised. We needed to get out of here soon.

We were fed up with not getting any information from Demelza, we were lucky if HG knew some of what was happening.

'Herbie, please explain why it might be your fault,' Jenna sat in the bar while we watched HG order himself another drink.

'Not Herbie, call me HG, please,' he said. 'It was in the pages from her book.'

I shot a look at Jenna which Demelza caught and smiled. We hadn't said anything. Masterson had handed it over to me. He had given in to his children, they might have had no idea what it was about, but having been saved from the bear they felt we deserved some reward, that and Jenna starting to pull bits of burning wood out of the fire in the hall.

'You have got it, I know you have.' Demelza was rubbing the back of her head. 'Let's see it.'

There didn't seem any point in keeping it hidden so I pulled it out from my jacket. It was just a few sheets held together by what was left of the cover.

'It's not really more than a school book,' Jenna said, after flicking through the pages. 'With pictures, not sure what you could do with that.'

'The ideas, can't you see the ideas?' HG pulled at the pages and several came away in his hand. 'Look at these guns and, what are they called, rockets and bombs. Look at these pictures of the houses in flames and the numbers of dead – millions.'

'That will happen whatever we do,' Jenna murmured.

'I will stop it.' HG tried to make that sound possible.

'This stuff about the nuclear bomb.' I poked my finger into the pages HG was holding and pulled them to the table. 'There's not a great deal of detail here. Surely not enough to make a real nuclear bomb?'

'HG is probably right, it is the ideas.' Jenna looked at the pictures. 'If you knew someone could make one, that it was going to happen, you'd put a lot of effort into trying. Especially if there was a war.'

'That's what did happen in the second war,' Demelza said.

HG shrieked, 'There's another one?'

We all nodded and HG ordered another drink.

'This still isn't getting us any closer to understanding why you,' Jenna gave Demelza a violent poke, 'why you wanted us dead and where you were going.'

Demelza said nothing. Jenna tapped me on the shoulder and pointed at the fire. It might be smouldering but I took hold of something that looked like you might use to roast marshmallows or whatever they roasted in this time, and put it into the glowing part of the fire.

'You wouldn't …' Demelza tried to look brave.

'Demelza, I will. I'm sick of trying to get you to talk. Alvin is going to get that thing hot and we are going to start burning bits of you.'

Demelza looked around the bar, 'They won't let you.'

'Of course not,' I said. 'That's why we are going to drag you outside first before we torture you. There are loads of metal things we can heat up.'

HG startled. 'Wait a minute, let me explain.' HG turned to the end of Miss Tregarthur's pages. 'It's here. I explained it to Demelza before.' He pointed and we all looked over.

After a second or two Jenna stabbed her finger on to a picture. 'The curry. That's not what Miss Tregarthur was shouting, not curry but Curie, Marie Curie. It says here she was the one who discovered Radium, radiation.'

I read a bit more. Jenna leant in before saying, 'But it's not now, we're too early, Marie Curie didn't invent this for another ten years or so.'

'That's why she went berserk when she found out what year it was, too early. That's why she's coming back,' I said. 'But how? And …' I turned to HG, 'Why didn't you tell us?'

'I thought Demelza was in danger,' HG blustered. 'I didn't know that she would hide information you needed to know.'

'Alvin, how hot is that iron?' Jen pointed at the fire.

'It's the radiation,' Demelza gave a huffed sigh. 'Miss Tregarthur wants the radiation. She believes she can get the crystal to work again if she exposes it to a high dose of radiation.'

'A high dose? Why a high dose?' Jenna asked.

'Because the usual dose wasn't going to work.'

'USUAL,' both Jenna and I shouted. The bar was at least empty now. Jenna grabbed Demelza's arm and twisted it hard.

Demelza screeched again but finally gave up and told us. 'There were other times,' Demelza said. 'Other times when she told us the crystal was fading.' She looked slyly at Jenna, this probably wasn't completely true.

'Then what?' I felt Demelza was stringing this out.

'She took us to another place on the moor,' Demelza said. 'A place where she said that radiation came out of the rocks. She used it to get the crystal recharged.' Demelza explained.

'And she didn't try it this time?' I asked.

'No, she said it was nearly dead, no use, she needed something stronger.' Demelza looked away. 'I didn't know that she was shouting about this Curie woman who discovered radium. I thought she was just stupidly ranting about curry.'

That's exactly what I would have thought so I couldn't really blame her. Jenna wasn't ready to give Demelza any credit: 'You might have told us,' and poked her once more.

'And what,' Demelza rounded on her. 'What would you have done after that? You'd have known all about this Marie Curie, would you? I don't think so. You don't know anything.'

This wasn't going anywhere, I butted in before a real fight started: 'Where has Miss Tregarthur gone now? If the crystal is dead?'

'She's taken it to the cave,' Demelza said.

Cave? There was always a cave involved. 'Why?'

'I don't know,' Demelza looked like she was trying to think rather than lie which had to be a better sign. She picked up Miss Tregarthur's pages. 'This says Marie Curie found radium in about ten years from now. Maybe she can't get the crystal to give her full control over the tunnel but perhaps she can get it to take her a few years forward, so she can get to the radium.'

'And if she can't get through time she'll have to work on the bomb with Masterson? Or at least use that scheme to get at something radioactive.' Maybe she doesn't actually need the bomb at all.' Jenna was still looking at the page, she flicked me a glance and a quick tilt of her head.

'Look,' I said loudly, drawing attention. 'Do we go after her or wait to see if she comes back?' I did wonder what we could have missed but I also needed to give Jenna a moment. I could see what she wanted to do.

'First we take Demelza back to that brothel and leave her there with HG,' Jenna said, with her serious frown.

'You still need me to find her cave,' Demelza squeaked. I didn't like to think what was in HG's mind.

'Why?' I couldn't see any point in finding another cave.

'Because if Miss Tregarthur can get her crystal to work a bit, we could do the same with the piece you've taken from me.'

It took a while for Demelza's suggestion to sink in.

'Before you do anything ...' HG snatched up the papers and chucked them on to the fire. 'At least I've stopped him making that awful bomb,' he said, as we watched them burn.

I didn't mind, it was all the pages except the one Jenna had snatched from the table.

I didn't like to tell him that if Miss Tregarthur returned she probably didn't need any pictured pages to start work on a nuclear explosion. She was a teacher after all. But that wasn't the only puzzle. 'I still can't see the problem. I mean if Masterson did make this bomb he's right, he could stop the war?'

'He might, but you might not like the result.' HG stepped

away from the fire and was looking for another drink.

'Why?' I asked.

'You said the war was started by the Germans.'

'Yep,' Demelza added and she knew what was coming. I think Jenna must have known as well.

'Germany is where the rest of Masterson's family live,' HG said. 'That's where he made his money, that's the country he would side with in a war. He has lots of Germans staying at his house from time to time. It's his business. That's why he has a German quote over his library door, I thought you understood that.'

'Absolutely,' I said, having no idea what he was talking about.

'Miss Tregarthur knows it too,' Jenna jumped up. 'It won't be us that wins the war, it's the other side. She plans to explode her nuclear bomb on Britain.'

'There will be no winners in such a war,' HG slurred with the alcohol working but I thought he was probably right.

'We have to get back to the moor,' Jenna said, looking outside. We'd managed to keep this bar going all night. A faint light shone in the sky. 'And we need to go now.'

-11-

Back to the Moor

Travelling about, in this time, was becoming familiar and long. We were back on the trains and two days later returned to the small horse-smelling grey town below the moor. HG couldn't believe that the rest of England was as foul smelling as we found it.

Onwards, again in another horse drawn carriage, we returned to the moorland village. At the inn the landlord still hadn't returned and the drinking men hadn't left. The landlady – Bettie – was still miserable although she gave me a small smile and HG a bigger one. She could see a smile at HG might be valuable.

We stayed overnight, ate more potatoes and answered none of their questions.

'She was here,' eventually Bettie told us that the nasty wild-haired woman had bundled through their little village, making demands and paying little. 'You're after her, I expect.' Bettie still hoped to get paid for more information.

'Yes,' HG said to her next smile.

'Well you'll be wanting to know which direction she took?' Bettie looked hopefully at him. HG handed her a tip rather too quickly.

'Up there.' Bettie pointed towards the moor and pocketed the money.

'Then?' asked HG.

'Cost you,' Bettie smiled yet again, it wasn't a great look.

I grabbed HG's arm, 'No need. It's time to go.'

We left, making for the tor above the village, along the ridge path. Finally, we were standing, once more, below the muddy brown of Hanging Stone Hill. A windy drizzle was the best weather the moor could give us that day. The walk had exhausted HG, or Demelza had exhausted him, asking for help and even to be carried. Jenna and I laughed when HG tried and only managed to drop her into a patch of something prickly.

We stopped for a while below the hill. Waiting and listening and watching for any movement. This felt dangerous. Miss Tregarthur might be up there. We hoped she would be, but how could we creep up on her?

Above us the hill was in open moorland. There were few other rocks at the top apart from the Hanging Stones, which stood a little below the peak. Last time she had been armed with a gun. Maybe she still was. We had to find her and stay alive.

Before we went on Jenna motioned to me with her head, for us to step aside, leaving Demelza and HG trying to shelter, the drizzle falling a little harder.

Jenna said quietly, 'Why did Demelza want us dead again? The bear? That was meant to kill us all.'

'No idea.' I looked back at Demelza and HG. It felt such a bad idea still having her with us. Demelza had always tried to get rid of us, ever since we'd been in this time travelling mess. Why was this different?

'But why now?' Jenna puzzled. 'And why did she want us

dead along with Masterson? Surely it was more likely the animal would kill him. It charged into his house, Demelza wouldn't have known we'd be in the hallway.'

I couldn't solve this. I did wonder if this time travelling had simply turned Demelza into a homicidal maniac. Perhaps she had always been like that, even at school, without having the chance to murder many people. Here she could slaughter as many as she wanted.

'We only have a small piece of the crystal,' Jenna took my hand. She did have an idea. 'Maybe Demelza believes that it could be too small, wouldn't have the power to make the tunnel take us all but might do it for just one person.'

'Could be, or perhaps she wants to make up with Miss Tregarthur in case she's the only one who can get this tunnel to work now.'

'Why do away with Masterson?' Jenna said. 'He was part of Miss Tregarthur's plan.'

'Not a great plan.' I thought of the pages from her book. 'Can't see building this bomb ever happening, too difficult.'

'It did in the end,' Jenna said. 'The nuclear bomb was built. Anyway, maybe Miss Tregarthur doesn't need the actual bomb, just radioactivity to bring this crystal back to life.'

No point in going over this, we had no explanation. Getting any more out of Demelza was a pain and even with violence I couldn't trust what she said. 'See what happens,' I said, before we re-joined the other two and walked on again.

Soon we were high enough to see the balanced Hanging Stones and we made our way to stand in front of them. HG seemed to think it was magical, he couldn't believe that the stones wouldn't break apart. He tried over and over again, making small grunts and wails. I worried that HG wasn't completely in touch with reality, but we *were* talking about time travel.

Jenna went and banged on the rocks, banged with the piece of crystal she had taken from Demelza, and nothing happened. We all took turns to do the same thing. Still nothing happened.

The drizzle turned to rain. We sheltered beneath the few overhanging rocks, ate some of the food Bettie had sold us – a potato pie – and we waited. It grew dark. We waited, hoping the tunnel might appear.

HG seemed to sink into himself, saying nothing and staring wildly at us. Perhaps it was our conversation, which had turned through all the weird things that had happened. As always we talked about the others who had been with us, some from the very start, some who had died and that stopped us talking altogether.

We slept, damp and restless. In the night I wondered about wolves but we heard nothing. As the light returned, mist started to rise up from the valley, a damp blanket that made me shiver.

Again Jenna went and hit the Hanging Stones with the piece of crystal. She smashed it down over and over again until her hands were raw and bleeding. Nothing happened.

Demelza joined her. 'We'll get it back for you,' she shouted. Her voice echoed across the moor. Nothing came from the stones. If the tunnel did have any life of its own, I doubted it would believe anything Demelza offered.

A weak sun appeared, but strong enough to chase away some of the mist. I stood and stretched, looking out on the moor. A fantastic place, if a bit wet. Those huge stones standing on the top of each tor, frowning down at the world. Standing watch over centuries of change, from the time of the cavemen to modern life, over people like we once were, children at school going for a hike.

I almost laughed thinking how it had all started. But here we were, stuck in a time that was not our own. It wasn't right, we had to get home somehow. Once, Jenna and I had the crazy idea of staying in a cave, trying to make a new life. It would never have worked. We just had to face all our problems at home. But how could we ever get there?

I joined the two girls and ran my hands over the rough stones. Their balance appeared so fragile. They didn't look natural, looked as though they had been made to confuse anyone who tried to pull them apart. HG certainly was confused and hadn't moved from our sheltering point. I started to go back to him.

'Is that …' Jen called out and knelt on the ground, '… another piece of her crystal?' she said, standing up and holding something in her hand. 'Does this mean the whole thing is breaking apart?'

As she stood, the piece she held glimmered in the light, giving off a stream of colours. Within seconds the colours dimmed.

'It's definitely part of her crystal,' Demelza crowded in on Jenna for a better look. 'She must have come here again. Used her iron bar and broken it again. Let me see.' Demelza leant forward with her hand open.

Jenna closed her hand on the new piece of stone and turned away. Demelza's face tightened in a grimace for a second.

I shuddered, remembering that awful sound coming from the tunnel when Miss Tregarthur had called it to obey her commands. To break the crystal would have been even more terrible, unless as Demelza had said, the thing had died – if a stone can die.

'You said it didn't work when she tried it last time – when she shot Zach,' Jenna said, after taking a few steps away.

Demelza nodded. I wondered what she felt about Zach. They had spent so much time together, time trying to have us put to death, but what sort of relationship was it? Demelza was so changeable, not the faithful sort at all, happy to flirt with anyone, including me.

'If she's not here, it must have taken her,' Demelza said.

'Does that mean she could have travelled to the right time? To meet up with Marie Curie?' I looked around to see if there were any other signs that she might have left, but we found nothing.

'We know the tunnel must have a mind of its own,' Jenna said to the stones as if talking to them. 'When we said we would get the crystal and bring it back. I could feel … as though something was alive in the rock.'

'We haven't done it, not brought the whole crystal, have we?' I put my arm around Jenna as her shoulders dropped, everything hopeless.

'Miss Tregarthur must have made the tunnel work again,' Demelza cried and swung herself up on to the top of the Hanging Stones. 'Come on tunnel, show yourself, we are still after her, we'll bring you the rest of your crystal.'

'Demelza, you think that's really going to work? If the tunnel had a mind it knows what you did, it's never going to trust you.'

Jenna was right, nothing happened. The stones across the moor carried on frowning at us, dark and threatening.

'We have to get off the moor,' I said, looking at the sky.

'Demelza,' Jenna stood right in front of her. 'If Miss Tregarthur has managed to get the rest of the crystal to work again, we have to try to do the same with these pieces.'

Demelza said nothing.

'That was your plan, wasn't it?' Jenna moved even closer. 'You were going to get us killed, and after that you would try to use the crystal piece for yourself.'

Demelza looked as though that was exactly what she had had in mind.

'You said Miss Tregarthur took you somewhere else. You have to take us there.' Jenna made her words sound like a threat. 'Right now.' When Demelza didn't respond she ended up on the ground in the mud with Jenna standing over her again. 'Take us there.'

Demelza sneered and said nothing.

'Leave her,' I said. 'Leave her and we'll go back to the inn. See what a few more nights out here does, see if she'll talk after that. She can't do anything if she doesn't have any of the crystal.'

Demelza's head flicked from side to side. More rain was coming. More wind. The moor was a bleak place that day. It made Demelza start talking in her whinging voice: 'I told you, we went somewhere.'

'You didn't actually tell us anything helpful,' Jenna said. 'Where exactly did you go? Last chance before we leave you here.'

'To this cave, like I said,' Demelza snivelled. 'She said it was near her home.'

'Miss T has a home?' I said, not believing there was anything normal about her. 'Thought she lived in hell.'

'Not far wrong,' Demelza went on. 'She took us to this cave. It wasn't her actual home. She said she couldn't go to her actual home … didn't explain. But we stayed in the cave. Odd place, wet and slimy.'

'Go on.' Jenna let Demelza sit up.

'The cave had a green glow at the back, a sort of light coming from the stones.' Demelza stood and tried to brush away the mud. 'It has to be some sort of radiation for the crystal.'

'Re-charging it, you thought?' Jenna asked.

Demelza nodded.

'Why didn't she just do that this time?' I said.

Demelza looked away. 'I did tell you, she said it was too late, that the crystal was no use, she couldn't get it to work again, it was dead. Look at the pieces you've found.'

Jenna took out the two pieces and held them up.

Demelza went on: 'There's no light inside. You could always see some light in the crystal and after being in the cave the light became stronger.'

'She needed something stronger.' Jenna held the pieces up again, peering into them, Demelza was right; there was no light coming from them.

'A nuclear bomb would certainly be stronger,' I said, gesturing the explosion, 'Boom.'

'Well, she's trying something.' Jenna put the crystal pieces in her jacket pocket. 'We can't stay here so we might as well go to Miss Tregarthur's cave. Come on Demelza, take us to it.'

'Maybe,' Demelza said, with her usual sly tone.

I thought she would try and make some sort of demand.

'Oh Alvin, it's torture time again,' Jenna sounded so serious and Demelza cringed. 'Just take us to it.'

'Ok. Ok. It's over there.' She pointed down the valley, down into the mist which had formed again.

Before we left I hung back and shouted one more time at the Hanging Stones. I kicked out at the rock, hurting my foot, and still nothing happened.

'Come on,' Jenna shouted.

Surely it must have been my imagination but I thought I heard a deep whispered sigh coming from somewhere deep in the moor. Just imagination. I joined the others and we slipped and slid down the hill in the mud. HG appeared to be a little better as we came down off the high moor.

-12-

Tregarthur's Cave

Demelza pointed out the route, down into the valley and along a stream. In the mist it was difficult to be sure of our direction.

'Follow the stream,' Demelza said.

For a while the wind blew the mist away and we saw the valley open up before us, hills looming on either side. This felt familiar, a wild place but one that I recognised. As we came lower we saw sheep.

'No hut,' I said, but my words were blown away. There was no shepherd's hut, no dead bodies as there had been before. Just the bleak moor, always watching us. I didn't believe that was imagination, this moor was alive, the stones, the crystal and whatever happened to time. Nothing I could see helped to fix time, there was nothing to see that wasn't the moor, nothing made by man.

Further down we started meeting people. There were other people walking on the moor. Should we worry about them? They didn't seem to be part of any plot, Miss Tregarthur's plot, they were just walking on the moor. I couldn't help staring at them – their clothes, amazing, like you would see in old pictures but here they were alive. They were all men; I suppose no women had taken up walking.

'Women not allowed, I expect,' Jenna said. 'Had to stay at home and work.'

I thought she was right but that didn't stop us staring at their clothes: heavy tweeds and short length trousers with long socks and boots and above all wearing TIES! Why would anyone wear a tie to go walking?

I hadn't really taken into account HG's clothes but they were similar to the other walkers. The three of us were in rough jackets and trousers and I knew we looked more like labourers than people walking for pleasure. Everyone we passed said hello to HG and ignored us. Actually they didn't so much say anything but tipped their hats. Because that was the other thing they were all wearing – hats. Mostly flat cap, some tweeds and some …

'They're like Sherlock Holmes,' Demelza squealed at one group, all with the same hats, exactly like we'd seen on TV programmes.

'Deer stalkers, they're called,' HG found his voice to tell us something he knew about. 'You've heard of Conan Doyle, have you?'

'Who?' we all asked together.

'The great author who wrote about Sherlock Holmes – you mentioned him so you must have read the books.'

'No, saw an old TV programme,' I said.

'Wasn't one of his stories about this moor and a big dog?' Demelza said.

'I heard he was thinking about writing a book about some hound that was meant to terrorise this moor. But only thinking about it.' HG stared at the ground looking worried. 'Perhaps I'll tell him he should write it. Have you got an idea for the title?'

'Hound of the Basket thingies, wasn't it?' Demelza said.

'Don't know, we've done huge dogs on this moor already,' Jenna answered. 'Don't want anymore.'

HG must have felt we'd stolen his famous writer for our weird future things. He didn't say anymore, but did tip his hat at other walkers.

We went on, down a steeper part of the valley. Coming off the wild part of moor we found a path, used by other walkers but overgrown with ferns and brambles crowding our way. Brambles with long spiky thorns which whipped our legs, ferns dripping with water. And above us, the likelihood that we would soon get a lot more water from the sky.

'Somewhere near here,' Demelza said, when Jenna asked her several times where the cave might be. The path moved closer to the stream, closer and muddier.

Demelza stopped and looked around. 'We have to cross over the stream, get off this path.'

The stream wasn't wide and should have been easy to cross, but HG slipped and slid half into the water, I had to haul him out. There was no path on the other side. I pulled off a branch and started to smash my way through, Jenna did the same. Doing anything useful was beneath Demelza who just hung on to HG.

'In case he falls again,' she said, with her usual smirk.

Still following the stream, we were going down into a gully with the ground becoming steeper and steeper on our side, forming a cliff covered with rocks and trees leaning over towards the stream, some trees had tumbled down making it even harder to make our way.

HG found the cave. Not on purpose. He stumbled and fell

headlong down a hole into water. Demelza had, of course, let go of him as soon as he started to fall. I had to pull him out again, he was soaked and muddy and I didn't want to even think about the smell, this stream was used by animals and not only for drinking.

Jenna was peering at an opening in the cliff side, partly covered by ferns and by one of the fallen trees. It had to be the entrance to Miss Tregarthur's cave. The dark rock of the moor was streaked with browns and reds and greens. Colours we had not seen before out here, except in the crystal.

Water streamed out of the entrance, coming from darkness further in and flowing down to join the main stream.

'There is a path,' Demelza pointed.

On one side, a narrow ledge led into the cave. Could this have been used recently, by Miss Tregarthur? I couldn't see any footprints but they would probably have been washed away. To get to the ledge we had to push through a mass of brambles, catching at us with every move we made.

Jenna stopped, plucking a piece of yellow thread from a thorn and turned to me with a question on her face.

'Could be,' I said.

'She wears a yellow cloak,' Demelza had been leading and looked back at the thread.

Difficult to believe anything from one yellow thread. If it did belong to Miss Tregarthur had she snagged herself going in or coming out? Did it mean she was further inside or had she left?

'We need … keep quiet,' Demelza spoke so softly I didn't catch all her words.

Keeping quiet was probably a good idea but it was unlike Demelza to make that sort of suggestion. 'Is there something else in there?' I pointed into the dark. 'Apart from the fact that Miss Tregarthur could be lurking with her gun.'

'I said we HAD to keep quiet,' Demelza whispered. 'Miss Tregarthur said we had to keep quiet or her family would hear.'

That sounded a lot worse. If we didn't find Miss Tregarthur we might find a whole hoard of her crazy family. What were her family doing out here on the moor and why did she want to avoid them?

'Maybe her family know all about her, and that's why she kept away,' I said.

'We've met two of them before and both were all bad,' Jenna said. 'Although she is probably the worst.'

Demelza didn't know more or didn't own up to knowing more, even with the threats she got from Jenna. That didn't mean she was telling the truth. Truth and Demelza never went together. Was it likely that people might live in here? There were no signs that anyone had spent any time here.

'We went in quite a way,' Demelza explained. 'The cave goes back a long way and comes out somewhere on another side, I'll show you where we stopped.'

Jenna turned on Demelza. 'If you didn't go far in, how do you know it comes out somewhere else?'

'I don't,' Demelza squeaked as Jenna poked her and she stumbled. 'She said it went on, Miss Tregarthur said it did.'

'Can't you leave her alone?' HG helped her up.

'Leave her alone? Not really,' Jenna said, with a stifled laugh. 'I may have to kill her soon.'

Demelza clung on to HG. 'You'll save me, won't you Herbie?'

HG looked more than confused, banter was lost on him.

We followed Demelza further along the ledge, ducking

under the dripping overhanging rock. After a few more steps the passage became wider with no vicious plants to avoid, still following a branch of the stream. The further we went, the darker it became, and we were soon splashing through pools of water and feeling our way.

With the light from behind almost completely fading, I thought we might have to find something to burn to light the way. But as we turned a corner a faint glow appeared, a faint green glow coming from the rocks and getting stronger as we moved along.

It wasn't bright enough to see our way clearly. I had ended up in front and missed the dip in the roof, banged my head hard and stumbled forwards into a larger, wider space.

'Another cave, another place,' I muttered in the gloomy light and rubbed my head.

We could see more because the back of this cave glowed with a stronger green light. Bright enough to see where we were, as our eyes grew accustomed to the light. Bright enough to see there were signs that someone had been here before. This cave had obviously been used fairly recently. At one side there was an old battered chair, a row of shelves, a blanket and a rough bed.

'This has been used recently,' Jenna held up a cup she'd found on a ledge. There were a few plates and more mugs. 'Someone's been here, can't tell how long ago.'

'I told you, we came here,' Demelza sounded as though we should be pleased.

'She's not here now,' I said, after checking the cave to make sure there weren't any places for Miss Tregarthur to hide.

'Let's suppose she was here, did something with the crystal, made it work and she's left, what do we do?' Jenna rounded on

Demelza. 'What did she do with the crystal? What did she do to get it working again? What should we do with these pieces?' Jenna pulled out the two fragments.

'I'm not sure,' Demelza was obviously trying to hide information, almost as though she couldn't stop doing it, couldn't tell the truth.

'Talk, or you go in the stream.' Jenna had grabbed her and was about to upend her into the water before she gave in. I stood in front of HG in case he decided to intervene but he probably wanted to know more as well.

'Hold on, hold on,' Demelza squirmed in Jenna's grip. 'She tried to stop us watching her but I saw what she did. She put it up there near the brightest green light.' Demelza pointed to a ledge higher up on the cave wall.

'Then what?' Jenna still held on to her and gave her a shake.

'Leave me alone,' Demelza struggled which made Jenna take a stronger hold around her neck.

'I can't breathe,' Demelza gurgled.

'You can still talk,' Jenna eased her hold a bit.

'Just let me go and I'll explain.' Demelza did pull away and stood rubbing her neck as though it was some terrible injury.

'Well?' Jenna said and was ready to grab her again. Demelza had a habit of keeping secrets, and Jenna was becoming much harder on her. Jenna would have been like that at school. I knew that Demelza lying was not the only problem.

'It seemed to take on the green colour,' Demelza said, still rubbing her neck.

'Go on,' I said, more loudly than I had expected and the noise echoed around the cave.

'Shh. I told you, we have to keep quiet,' Demelza recovered, preferring giving instructions to being attacked.

I wasn't sure we should do anything Demelza told us. If we put the pieces up on the ledge, then Demelza might try and run off with them. It could just be a trick.

If Miss Tregarthur's family lived somewhere round here, and if she was so keen to avoid them, they might even help us. Having thought that, I remembered Hugh – one of her relatives who'd locked us in a barn to wait for the hanging party. I shivered, probably best to keep quiet.

'When Miss Tregarthur put the crystal up there it turned green as though the stone was regaining its power?' I asked.

'That's what I said.' Demelza looked pleased, happy to be the one who knew most.

'She must have come back here after she left that Masterson man.' Jenna reached up to the ledge and ran her hand along it, not finding anything.

'I just don't understand why she didn't do it straight away, why all this messing around with nuclear bombs and radiation? Why didn't she come here straight away?' I said.

'I told you she kept saying it was no use this time,' Demelza said.

'What could have changed her mind? What happened to make her decide this was worth a try?' Jenna could have been asking the cave for all the answers I had.

HG had not said a word since we had been in the cave. In the silence after Jenna's question he coughed and said: 'This time travel is probably rubbish, I don't believe a word you've been saying, but you did say you thought she'd got it wrong, didn't you? Came to the wrong time.'

'Of course … she didn't know,' I started. 'When she came

out of the tunnel, shot Zach and went off, she thought it was the right time, the time she had planned to find Marie Curie.'

'She must have known the crystal was fading. She knew that before she came here,' Jenna said.

'That's right …' Demelza blurted before realising this was another new piece of information.

'Maybe the tunnel did it on purpose.' Jenna just held off another attack on Demelza. 'It planned to let her rot in this time, no crystal, no time travel. Miss Tregarthur sets up Masterson just in case, in case she is stuck here.'

Demelza gave a sort of nod as though she agreed with Jenna. If so, that meant she knew it already, I couldn't see how she could have worked it out.

'She only needs to jump a few years forward,' Jenna sounded as though she had the answer. 'Doesn't need to make the crystal work perfectly, just enough to get her to Marie Curie. That's why she came here.'

There seemed a lot of holes in that explanation, but it was probably the best we could do. 'Are we trying to go after her or to get home?' I wasn't clear what Jenna felt we should be doing.

'We're still trying to get this crystal to the tunnel in the hope that the tunnel will take us home, it won't do that unless we bring the crystal,' Jenna said, making it clear that this was still what we had to do.

'Even if it doesn't … even if it's dead?' I said, realising how daft that sounded, talking about a dead piece of stone.

'Yep.'

'Ok,' I agreed, looking down at the rough bed. We could be here for a while and I wished we could find somewhere a bit more comfortable.

'Demelza, tell us again what she did here. When you weren't passing the time plotting our deaths, what exactly did she do?' Jenna stepped closer.

'Told you, she put the crystal up there,' Demelza pointed back to the ledge.

'And?'

'Then she'd take it away and say it was no use and she'd find another space. Like that one,' Demelza pointed to another hole in the wall. 'She'd do it over and over, saying it wasn't powerful enough. But in the end she seemed happy enough.'

'Happy with what?' I said.

'When she took it out the crystal colours were brighter, all sorts of colours.'

'There, that wasn't too difficult,' Jenna prodded her. 'Wasn't too difficult to tell a bit of the truth, was it?'

Demelza pouted. 'When it didn't work quickly, Miss Tregarthur often said she needed something more powerful than this cave.'

'Perhaps she'd had the nuclear bomb idea before,' Jenna said.

'Why Masterson? Where does he fit in?' I said, after a while.

'Wasn't he in the book?' Demelza said.

'No,' HG butted in, startling us. 'It was just those machines of war.' He'd said so little since we'd been in the cave. But Masterson still remained a mystery. How had Miss Tregarthur known about him?

We put the broken pieces of crystal on the ledge and waited. As Demelza said, our stone took up the green glow. The glow disappeared when we took the pieces away from the light.

'Leave them overnight. That was what Miss T did,' Demelza suggested.

That sounded a reasonable idea, but it could just be Demelza planning to steal the pieces when we slept. I could see Jenna had the same idea in her mind.

The stifling air in the dark, cold cave eventually drove us outside. A few steps away from the cave entrance the stream opened up onto a grassy area. I tried to light a fire but didn't succeed. It was a cool night but none of us wanted to sleep in the cave. HG shivered and groaned all the time.

None of us slept for long, occasionally I or Jenna stumbled back in the dark to check if anything had happened to our pieces of crystal. Nothing had happened.

'Not you,' Jenna said, when Demelza tried to do the same.

-13-

The Sound of the Moor

In the morning we took the crystal pieces to the darkest place in the cave.

'Maybe,' I said, looking at them.

'Maybe not,' Jenna peered again.

We talked ourselves into believing there was a faint glow from our pieces of stone. We stared at them for so long it could just have been our imagination. Out in the daylight there was probably nothing to see.

'We have to go up there again,' Jenna pointed a weary arm up towards the moor and the Hanging Stones. 'I suppose it might work.'

HG was muttering to himself. Was he going crazy? Were we making his world too strange, too weird, for him? He still followed as we set off.

There were no cap tipping walkers on the moor at such an early hour and the darkening sky was unlikely to persuade them ever to set out. The moor was set for another downpour, blown by the usual gale. We were soaked, exhausted and hungry by the time we reached the stones.

Getting there had taken most of the day. Stopping and

searching for shelter each time the rain and wind grew too strong to see where we were going. The food was gone but there was enough water, a lot of water everywhere.

As we neared the hill, my thoughts grew more miserable: surely nothing would happen; would we stay forever out here on the moor; could there be any hope?

Standing in front of the strange stones Demelza stamped her feet as water ran down her face. 'Now what are you going to do?'

Jenna ignored her and took out the crystal pieces. She held them in her hands like an offering. 'We are here to help,' she called out against the wind. Nothing. Jenna tried again. Nothing. She kicked out at the Hanging Stones. Nothing. Her head dropped as she cried, 'Help us.' Still nothing happened.

The rain fell harder, streams of water ran down the hill, clouds of mist drove into our faces, whipped by a wind almost too strong for us to stand in without holding tight to the rocks. It felt as though the moor was against us, everything was against us.

HG stood in a silent trance, not speaking, his clothes soaked, he closed his eyes.

'Hit them, hit them, just hit them,' Demelza shouted.

Jenna turned the two pieces in her hand. Not quite stone, nor crystal, showing no light inside. She shook her head. We remembered the terrible sound when Miss Tregarthur had smashed the iron bar against her crystal, too awful to hear again, although I knew we would have to do it in the end.

Demelza did it for us. Lurching forward, she snatched the pieces from Jenna and smashed them together. Nothing happened. Absolutely nothing, just more rain and wind. No sign, no light, no howl of pain.

Only one other group of rocks on this hill provided any shelter and we huddled under them. It might be pointless to stay here, but also pointless to leave. I placed the pieces of crystal on top of the stones. Even in this gloomy morning they sparkled, but sparkled only with the sun's weak light. There was no trace of green or red or any other colour.

Soon any sparkle faded because this daylight was moor-dark, towering storm clouds blotted out the sun, wind whistling across the moorland. The streaming mist cleared briefly to give glimpses of bleak tors in this empty wilderness. Dark hills almost telling me what was coming.

I shivered. We should not be here. I tried to cry out, no words came. I had felt this before, something gathering force, gathering strength.

From far away a thunderous noise rolled towards us, sweeping over the moor and from the earth below came the crushing and grinding of rock against rock. The ground heaved, groaning as the hillside started to tear itself apart, boulders toppling and tumbling into huge cracks that opened around us.

The earthquake had come for us again.

This time there was nowhere to run except to the Hanging Stones, the only rocks that didn't move. Jenna and I pulled HG to his feet, together we staggered over to cling to the balanced rocks. Demelza made it on her own.

The noise pounded in my head, louder and louder. Through the earthquake a new sound broke through, almost human, as though a voice spoke from the very ground, a voice from this earthquake, a voice of the moor. One word echoed out and that was 'DEATH.'

Jenna held out our pieces of crystal. 'STOP,' she yelled. 'STOP,' she screamed at the stones. 'We are on your side, here to help, to get the rest of the crystal, to bring back Miss Tregarthur and finish this.'

Jenna's voice faded on the wind. We had failed. More cracks ran across the ground. Huge chasms opened up, chasms of molten rock, jets of flame spurting into the air. Hanging Stone Hill had become a place of burning hell. We held on, but my grip started to fail and soon we would fall to our end in the fire below.

'HALT,' a new voice tore into the air. 'By the stones, by the earth, by the water I call upon you to stop, to return to peace.'

I turned. Above us an ancient man stood shouting out his commands. His robe shone out even in the gloom; reds and purples and greens, so many colours. I could feel the force in his words, fighting the moor, fighting the earthquake, fighting the lifeform of time that wanted to bury us.

Again and again, the man shouted. With each of his shouts the raging storm paused, but it was only to start again seconds later with even more force. Still the man shouted. In his bony hand he held an iron staff. It seemed to take all his strength but he lifted it and crashed the staff against the hillside. 'I tell you to stop in the name of time. You will stop.'

Even though his voice quietened to a gasp, his power won through. The hillside had been broken, split by enormous fissures, but with each crash of his staff the land started to heal, to come together again. The moment passed, the danger passed, the battle was over. The gale slowed, the rain turned to drizzle, the clouds scattered. The moor became the moor again.

The man steadied himself, leant heavily on his staff. There was something familiar about him, more familiar than I liked. A man with the same wild hair of someone we had met – Miss Tregarthur.

'Alvin Carter,' the old man called to me.

I didn't move, I still held on to these granite rocks. Instantly I was taken back to the crowd chasing us in the time of the Black Death. A crowd driven mad by a priest who wanted to see us burn. This man looked like that priest, his robe had faded to white, the colours disappearing.

I was ready to run.

'Stay,' cried the man as though he knew exactly what I was going to do. 'I will let you go across time, to follow Alice. To stop her. To bring her back and return the crystal.'

That might sound better than burning but I wasn't sure this man really had a better offer.

'We want to go home,' Jenna moved from the stones towards him.

The man raised his staff, threatening. 'And you will.'

'You mean we might get home providing we do what you tell us.' Jenna stood right in front of him. 'You're one of them aren't you, one of the Tregarthur lot, why can't you sort her out?'

The man stepped back. His face showed no emotion but I could see he was really ancient, his face cracked and lined, his body thin and wasted. I saw what Jenna had seen, features like those of Miss Tregarthur. Family. He might be one of the Tregarthurs but he was in no state to do anything. The battle with the moor had almost killed him.

'It is for you to do.' The man waved his arm in my direction.

'This has started with you and must end with you.'

'How?' Jenna pointed to the Hanging Stones. 'There is no tunnel. Can you control it?'

'I cannot control her, she has so much fury now she sees no hope.' He paused and I wondered why he called the time tunnel 'her', but he went on. 'I ask, that is all I can do. You know Alice has something she needs, you have a part of it in your hand.'

He looked towards Jenna holding our pieces of the crystal. 'I will ask her to take you where you must go. This is your last chance.'

Jenna had questions and fear on her face. The moor was so quiet, but the threat of death in the earthquake made it hard to focus on his words. Or was that it? He had a force I did not understand. I wanted to agree, not to argue. Hadn't we planned to go after her anyway? We were so many years away from anything like home, we had nowhere else to go.

He had said this was our last chance.

'No choice,' I said to Jenna before turning to the old man. 'Show us what to do.'

HG still stuck to the rock, his eyes closed again, not responding to the man or his words. Perhaps he believed we'd arrived somewhere in his future already. If this was his view of the future, it had been a terrible vision. Would he ever recover?

Demelza stood with her mouth open and moved a little closer to HG, taking his hand. I guess she was trying to work out what might be best for her – just for her.

'First you also have something I need,' the man said to me.

'Around your arm you have a belt of gold.'

How did he know so much about us? Would he explain? There was an urgency about him. The moor still gave occasional tremors, the clouds had not gone far, as though this pause might not last for long. It wasn't going to be a time for explanations.

'You must give me the belt.' He held out his hand. 'You must. It must go back in history. Back in time.'

I drew away, confused. 'It's the only thing we can use for money if we go after her.'

The man took a purse from beneath his robe. 'You can use this and if you need more you will find Masterson will help.'

'Masterson?' How did he know of Masterson? 'He won't help.' I didn't want to meet up with that man again, he'd probably shoot me next time.

'Masterson will help,' the man gasped. 'Masterson has to help. You must go to him.'

That could explain a lot. Miss Tregarthur had found Masterson. He had to be part of this awful story. A part we did not understand.

'If you know everything,' Jenna said, obviously getting angry. 'Why do you need us? Are you any better than Miss Tregarthur?'

'Maybe I'm not,' he said. 'But I'm giving you the only option you have, unless you're going to stay here. Bring her to me and then you can go home. Now GIVE ME THE BELT.'

'Why can't we go home now?' Jenna was used to people shouting at her and she just pointed at the Hanging Stones. 'Tell it – her – to send us home right now.'

Would he agree? Could we escape and leave all this behind?

Almost as soon as the words left her mouth I knew it wouldn't happen. There was a stronger judder in the land, another crack opened, the sky turned a little darker.

'Calm,' the man raised his staff again and shouted. 'They will go. They will find her, they will bring your crystal home.'

He was adding to the mystery. Was all this his invention? What gave him power over the time tunnel? He had made it clear that we no other option, do what he said or the earthquake would finish us.

'The belt, quick, hurry,' he said, twisting his head at the sound of another crack from the ground.

The gold belt had always been a problem. Given to me by the King of England in the time of the Black Death. Too valuable for us to change for money without making people believe we were thieves. Unwinding the belt from my arm, I handed it to him and took his purse.

The man weighed the belt in his hand before shouting once more: 'Go on, on, on,' and he waved us forward. 'And take this too.' He threw a small leather bag to me. 'Food.'

A faint trace of smoke rose from around the stones – the time tunnel was opening. We started to walk forward. The man was still shouting for us to hurry, his voice becoming hoarse and faint. Demelza held HG's hand and pulled him forward.

'Not him,' the man found the strength to scream.

Then I remembered. We had never been able to take anyone from their own time into the tunnel. When Lisa had wanted to take the baby Neanderthal Zog, he went berserk.

'He cannot go,' the man snatched HG's hand from Demelza. HG sagged to the ground, quivering.

'Take Demelza,' Jenna shouted to the man. 'Take her. We

don't want her. Take her.'

'She is part of this. I cannot take her, you must go,' the man croaked. 'Go now.'

We moved forward as though under his control. Was this urgency real or was it just to send us away without having to tell us any more? It was too late to find out. A mist started to flow out from the Hanging Stones, all sorts of colours. Soon it covered us and we could no longer see the old man or HG.

The swirling motion of the time tunnel took us, a funnel of twisting air. Flashing images tumbled past me, things we had seen, others we hadn't. Before I could focus on what I saw, everything stopped. The mist cleared.

We had arrived, back on the moor which seemed unharmed, no earthquake cracks, no falling boulders, the hillside unchanged. Again a wet drizzle in the air, but no old man and no HG, just us three. Maybe some of the huge stones had moved a little, maybe that was my imagination.

Jenna looked at Demelza. 'We should have left her.'

I tried to put my arms around Jenna but she shied away. Demelza rolled her eyes and I hoped Jenna didn't see that, or see the look Demelza gave me. There were more reasons to get rid of Demelza than being stuck in a time travelling nightmare.

We walked down from the hill, dazed since leaving the tunnel. As we walked we shared bread and cheese from the bag the old man had given us. Good enough to eat, but how much I would have given for something to eat from our own time. Would we ever get home? What could have happened while we were away? There were still so many problems to face. This was no time to think about home, we hurried to get off the moor, a familiar route. Back to the village.

The village and the inn had changed. An electric light shone in one of the windows. It might be a familiar place and a little more modern, but it was still in our past. We didn't stop, there was enough dark daylight to push on. Did we know where we were going? Maybe not, but we knew who we were going after.

-14-

New Clothes, New Plans

'Do we go to the first Masterson house we went to?' I said, as we walked down from the village.

'Do we go to him at all?' Jenna was picking her way between muddy puddles.

'That white robed man said we had to go to Masterson,' Demelza seemed to feel she had a more important role in whatever we were doing.

'Shouldn't have kept you with us at all,' Jenna glared at her. 'Maybe you could go away and find another bear to play with.'

'He said you had to take me, said I was part of this, you have to take me, he said so,' Demelza whined.

'Didn't say we had to be nice to you,' Jenna said, giving her a shove.

Demelza tripped and fell into a ditch full of nettles at the side of the road. Jenna looked at me, to see whether I'd help her up. A challenge. I didn't help, didn't dare help.

'Back to London.' Jenna walked off, leaving Demelza to scramble up and follow.

We didn't stop in the small town and made straight for the station.

1903, I saw the year on a poster.

With the money from the purse, we travelled more comfortably but it was still much the same as before – smoky trains and horse drawn carriages.

We had to stay in Exeter at the same inn, which now had toilets and sanitation, everything was a little cleaner although piles of horse dung still littered the streets. The next train we took to London was faster, people talking and saying how good modern travel had become. The train steamed across the countryside quite as fast as anything I'd been on back home.

People were moving all over the country and at first we didn't stand out. Nobody seemed interested in us, a few questions, a few thieves but we weren't an easy looking group so we were mostly left alone. Electricity was the new thing, not completely new but taking time to be installed across the country, there were still a lot of gas lights.

London was different, more cars, with more breakdowns and more arguments with the men on horses and even more noise. Here our working clothes did make us stand out, especially since we weren't working and weren't really sure what we were doing.

Demelza persuaded us to dress more for the time: 'Can't do anything with people staring at us.'

She pushed me into a man's shop, a very brown shop – brown window frames, brown door, brown counters. Just the clothes were black or grey or tweedy black and grey.

I ended up in heavy trousers and the same sort of clothes that most of the men had been wearing in the city when we had been in London before. That included a hat. A man in the shop said I had to wear one that looked like a pork pie on my head, no chance. I went for one more like a gangster. We had an argument about ties as well. He almost spat at my open shirt, but it stayed that way.

The girls could have had more fun. Jenna went for a long skirt, white shirt top with a flowered scarf and shoes she could actually walk in. Demelza spent ages and money. I really did not want to tell her, but the money spent was worth it.

Jenna huffed, Demelza preened and whirled. With Demelza's tastes, the money we had wouldn't last long, we would have to go to Masterson anyway.

'I've got you a hat,' Demelza whipped out a bonnet topped with feathers. 'Everyone's wearing them.' She plonked it on Jenna's head, her own hat was even larger.

We had arrived this time in early summer, warmer weather, hotter in the town. It made me feel that the girls were better dressed for this. I was sweating in heavy tweed and wondering about deodorant.

This time we went for a smarter hotel, not actually very smart, just more expensive. We had two rooms. Jenna and Demelza in one, me in the other. Room sharing with Jenna was definitely out. There was even a notice which said the management refused to take couples, unless married. There were a lot of notices. Even one that said you had to pay a fine if you wet the bed. No dogs.

We sat having tea in china cups in a fancy room at the hotel. Demelza told us that the decoration was chintz. It looked dangerous to me, ornaments and lace everywhere, the sort of things I could end up knocking over. And I was looking really really stupid in my suit although Demelza said I fitted in and she was right. All the men looked really really stupid. And sweaty. I forgot to take off my hat, a waiter coughed at me.

'What now?' Demelza's new confidence was annoying and we didn't answer. 'Go on, you must have a plan.' We still said nothing.

I ate a cake and wished I hadn't. It was fine on the plate, tasted like sawdust. We still said nothing.

The only thing we had to go on was the one page taken from Miss Tregarthur's book. The page that Jenna had hidden when HG threw the others into the fire. Only Jenna and I knew we had it and I didn't want to share anything with Demelza. For lots of reasons.

It didn't matter.

'Look,' Demelza butted into our silence. 'You've got that piece of paper, the one you think I don't know about, let's see it.'

'Fine.' Jenna slapped it on the table, rattling the cups. I held onto the plate of cakes.

It didn't tell us much. Someone called Marie Curie had discovered radium. The page gave the name of a laboratory but no address. There might have been more but we only had the one page with a picture of her and her husband.

'It doesn't sound English,' Demelza was still the only one doing any talking. 'French?' Demelza went on: 'The fashion looks French,' said our expert in clothes.

There was a sudden bang and a cloud of smoke outside the hotel. I leapt up, this trip had made me jump at loud noises.

'Just a car backfiring,' Jenna held my arm and I sat down again.

'And look at the car!' Demelza squealed as a very large, shiny and noisy vehicle passed the window.

'When were cars invented?' I had no idea, it was something to say to hide my embarrassment.

'About now, I guess,' Jenna said, and we fell silent again. Jenna and I needed to have this talk on our own, we needed to get rid of Demelza and she knew it and I didn't think she was going anywhere. She surprised us.

'You aren't going to tell me anything,' Demelza said. 'Not going to say anything with me here, so give me some of the money and I'll meet you back here in an hour.' We didn't have watches but there were clocks on many of the buildings.

Jenna and I exchanged eyebrow raising looks and a shrug. Jenna told me to do what she had asked. I handed her one of the white £5 notes.

'That should keep her busy,' I said, as she left.

'Don't count on it,' Jenna shook her head. 'What's she up to? No point in asking if we trust her because we don't.'

'I guess it's best we keep her with us, might get some warning. You're right she will be planning something.' I could still see Demelza walking down the street, looking in shop windows.

'You can stop watching now,' Jenna tapped me on the arm.

'I …'

Jenna leant in and kissed me on the cheek. 'It's ok.'

That made me blush and the waiter coughed again. Kissing was another thing not allowed.

'Let's go and check out Masterson's house.' Jenna stood up. 'Come on.'

We had picked this hotel hoping it was in the part of London we remembered. After asking a few questions in the hotel we found out Masterson's house wasn't far away. He was even more well-known than before, his house in an expensive part of town.

His road looked much the same as before, some different street lights, bigger trees, less smell – probably even more expensive since our last visit.

Outside the house there were several horse drawn covered wagons. They were being loaded from a door at the side.

'He's moving,' I said, pointing at the chests, furniture and statues being carefully packed.

'What now?' I said, as we stood across from the building which I still felt should be a town hall.

'See what happens.' Jenna pointed; there was Demelza crossing the road, looking from side to side, not for horses or cars, she was checking who was watching her. I suppose she didn't notice us in our new clothes, we fitted in.

We saw Demelza reach up and use the door knocker. A great big brass knocker that we could hear from across the road. A man appeared in the same uniform as we had seen before. Demelza started arguing, the man started to close the door on her, she pushed against it.

'Go away,' we heard the man say loudly as he shoved her backwards and did push the door shut. Demelza turned around with her best cross face. I waved and she looked even more cross. We went over to her.

'Hopeless,' Demelza said.

'I thought you were going shopping.' Jenna gave a half smile.

'I was … just happened to end up here so I thought I'd knock, see if he was in.' Demelza gave an expected lie.

'What did that man say?' I asked.

'Told me to go and not in a very nice way,' Demelza said, in her spoilt little girl voice.

Jenna spun her round while saying, 'Did you tell him anything?'

'No … no … of course not … what should I have said?'

'You should have waited for us,' Jenna snapped.

'You didn't tell me that. Anyway you've no idea what to do, have you?' Demelza pulled away.

We were starting to draw attention to ourselves. The wagon loading men had stopped loading.

'Try again,' I said, to stop the argument and stepped up to the door. I banged loudly, very loudly.

That brought the man back, he saw Demelza. 'I told you, go away, no hawkers, no work, go away.'

I wondered what a hawker was, but not for long because I wasn't going to let him close the door. I shoved. He didn't expect that and stumbled backwards shouting for help. We piled into the large hallway. Most of the statues had been taken away. More servants appeared, six of them. They were ready to throw us out.

'Where's the bomb, Masterson?' I shouted and my voice echoed against the marble. 'Is Alice Tregarthur here?'

That didn't stop the servants, who were already pushing us towards the door.

The library door opened and Masterson came slowly out. Older, balder, fatter than before, with lines on his face – worried lines.

'You,' he blustered. 'You,' he repeated. 'You … came back.'

'Moving are you? Thought you could run?' I said, shrugging off one of the servants who had tried to take my arm. It was obvious we knew his master and he wasn't sure if he still had to throw us out.

The lines on Masterson's face sagged and I knew I was right. 'That's what you're doing, running, moving out. Has

Miss Tregarthur been here?'

Again his face gave away the truth.

'And you haven't made her bomb, have you?' Jenna's turn to say her bit. 'Where's she gone now? What's making you leave in such a hurry?'

It wasn't just his face that sagged as Masterson said, 'You'd better come in here,' and he turned back into the library. We pushed through the servants and followed. Masterson sat heavily on a chair as we came in.

'She's going to ruin me,' he almost cried with his head in his hands.

I looked at Jenna, then at Demelza, before it came to me. This fitted with what HG had told us about Masterson. Miss Tregarthur would use it. 'She's going to tell everyone you are a German spy isn't she?'

From the look on his face there were two obvious facts. One I was right, but more importantly it was true. He really was a spy.

'You're leaving the country, aren't you? And I guess you did have a copy of the pages from Miss Tregarthur's book? You've handed them over to your friends in Germany. Am I right?'

Masterson couldn't stop his face giving him away. Surely he couldn't have been a very good spy?

'The bomb?' Jenna let that hang in the air.

Masterson sat forward. 'They don't believe in the bomb, no one believed me, I tried …' He suddenly realised what he was about to say, to say that he tried to get people to believe in a nuclear bomb that might have been dropped on London.

'What did they believe?' I wondered what sort of spying he had actually been doing. What other ideas in Miss Tregarthur's pages had been more believable?

It was clear that Masterson must have felt he had said too much. 'What do you want?'

I think he realised who he was talking to, realised he didn't have to be scared of us at all. He recovered his snarl. In a moment of transformation he changed from the cowardly man I had met before, into someone who felt their own importance.

'What is it that you want?' he said. 'I'm a very busy man.'

'Probably we want to save the world,' Jenna started and then said: 'But for now, we need to know what's happened to Alice Tregarthur.'

'And we need more money,' Demelza added.

With his confidence restored he was harder to deal with. He was in his mansion, surrounded by his servants, a successful man, who were we? Demelza asking for money was simpler to deal with than answering our questions.

He thought he would be able to pay us off. That was probably what he was more used to doing. His money was his power. He gave no answers when we pressed on German war plans, but was quite happy talking about money. We should not have let that happen.

Any threat of exposing him as a spy was laughed off, we had no proof, just suspicions. Perhaps Miss Tregarthur had some real proof, but we had none. Masterson might have kept a copy of the pages from her book, pages about weapons. But we couldn't prove anything.

So it was strange when he made another offer of help: 'You need to find Alice Tregarthur and take her back, you say? I really can help you with that.'

Whoa, what had he just said? We had not mentioned anything

about taking her 'back' anywhere. I could see he would like the idea of removing Miss Tregarthur. That would stop her denouncing him as a spy but we hadn't said anything about taking her back.

'Where is this 'back' place?' I thought I had caught him out.

'I'm afraid I can't talk about that,' was his answer and his only answer when we asked him what he knew about the moor, the robed man, or the Hanging Stones.

'Can't talk or won't talk?' Jenna pushed him.

'Both.' And that for him was an end of the discussion. He rang for his butler, offered us lemonade. We might have saved his daughter from the bear but in this room we were the children.

'The robed man said you would help us?' I tried not to whine but I didn't succeed. Masterson might be of no use with bear attacks but here in his library he made me feel useless.

'And I will help.' I think he added 'dear boy' but my head was swimming. Even Demelza was awfully quiet.

Masterson stood, walked to his fireplace, put a hand on the mantelpiece and turned to us as though giving a lecture. 'She's gone to France. Told me she has to find Marie Curie in her laboratory. Said she has to have something called radioactivity.'

I would have liked to throw him into the flames but the fireplace was empty, no fire.

Masterson went on, 'You will need to go there too. I will have my secretary make the arrangements.' He rang the bell again. 'We won't need to meet again.' He started for the door which opened and his secretary came in.

'Ah, Derek,' Masterson said. 'Look after them, will you?'

'Hang on.' I jumped up.

'Yes?' he said, as though I was being annoying.

I couldn't think of anything. Masterson stopped at the door. 'If you get that woman, just contact Derek.'

'And if we don't?' Jenna plonked herself down in Masterson's chair.

'Well, if you don't … well, it's too bad … just too bad, but don't come here again.' Masterson disappeared through the door.

We were left with Derek who had a foreign accent. He told us he would make all the arrangements for us to go to France.

'Do we need passports?' Demelza asked, sounding as though this was a holiday trip.

'No. Passports are not needed,' Derek's clipped voice dealt with all our questions. 'I will bring tickets to your hotel tomorrow.' He stood, obviously we were being dismissed.

We didn't trust any of these people but what else could we do? I wondered if Masterson would just vanish to Germany without doing anything for us. My hope was that the robed man on the moor had some power over him, but it was only a faint hope.

We were a pathetic group walking out into the hall which echoed with our footsteps now that everything had been removed. I felt as though we'd just had a visit to the head teacher. Something that always went badly for me.

Another door opened. A girl ran out, flung her arms around Jenna, then turned and did the same to me.

'I'll make sure he looks after you,' she said, before we heard a voice calling 'Julie'.

I only just recognised the girl we had saved from the bear. Masterson's brave daughter, now older. We left and walked to our hotel. We hadn't told Derek where we were staying and he hadn't asked.

A few streets later Demelza stopped and pointed. 'Hang on. That's the place, the coffee shop, the one we went to with HG. I bet he's in there.' She made for the door.

'Wait,' I called. I wasn't sure we wanted to meet HG again. We'd dumped him on the moor with the white robed man. What would he do if he saw us, even if he was inside?

The coffee shop hadn't changed much, still with posters outside with wonderful claims about their coffee. Demelza didn't wait but strode through the door. Jenna and I stayed outside.

It wasn't long before we heard the screams and Demelza ran out on to the street.

'He's barmy.' Demelza dragged us off, running.

'What happened?' I asked.

'He was there, sitting with all his mates at a table, He must have become more famous because they were all listening to every word he said, some even writing them down. I sat down near to him and he didn't recognise me at first. Must have thought I was another groupie fan. He was going on about another book he's writing.'

We'd made it to the end of the street. Demelza looked back, no one was following.

'Go on,' Jenna said.

We weren't used to Demelza telling us things – without the threat of torture – but she obviously wanted to tell us all about this.

'I took a cup of coffee from the table – much better, the sugar actually dissolved. And I was going to tap him on the shoulder and ask him how he was, but I didn't have to. One of the men started praising HG's time machine book, saying how wonderful it was. So I said, loudly, "Oh you did write it then?" Well, he turned to me and lost it when he realised who I was.'

Demelza resorted to giggling. 'He went on about how I'd tricked him, how he'd met up with people in white gowns and been put in a dungeon. But he was gabbling away and slowly wound himself into a terrible state and started throwing things, so I got out.'

'I guess the white robed man on the moor scared him off.' It made me laugh as well, not really fair on poor old HG, but I had to remember he wasn't quite as nice as he might have been. Probably should be in jail after that brothel incident.

'Perhaps we had better read his book,' Demelza was still giggling. 'We might be in it.'

-15-

PARIS

Trusting Derek, or at least having some faith in Masterson's daughter, meant we were waiting in a small room at the hotel called the 'salon'.

'Lounge,' Demelza told me.

The restaurant chintz had run out before they got to this room. The walls were yellow and the carpet green. Overall it gave a feeling of nausea. We sagged in heavy arm chairs, the sort you wouldn't expect a guest to damage or even move from their positions around the room, arranged like a waiting room, and we waited.

Derek arrived, clearly he hadn't needed us to tell him where we were staying. I suppose they were in the business of spying. Derek sat down and sniffed at us. He obviously thought it was beneath him to deal with people like us. 'You must do exactly as I say,' he said, with his accent getting stronger. He wasn't really any older than we were, and we'd met more frightening people.

'No we don't,' Jenna shook her head.

'You must …' Derek looked at each of us and frowned.

'You tell us what you have planned and we'll tell you if that's what we are going to do.' Jenna lifted herself on to the arm of her chair, a stronger position looking down on him.

Derek flapped, 'Mr Masterson says you have to do this.'

'We don't have to do what he says either,' I joined in. 'If we don't like it, we'll have to go and have another chat with him.'

That hit home. The last thing Derek wanted was us to go back to his employer, it would make him look ineffective. Masterson didn't want to see us again.

'It's alright, Dick.' Jenna patted him on the arm.

'Derek,' he corrected her and jerked away.

'Sure Der...ick, let's hear what you've planned.'

Derek moved us to a table at the side of the room. Another heavy piece of furniture. We stood around as he put documents down and tried to explain. Jenna kept interrupting, she was enjoying this.

'It is best you go on a tour, with a company.' He showed us a brochure. It was an English company which arranged trips to France. 'They take groups to visit Paris, see the Eiffel Tower, museums and art galleries.'

'Why don't we just go on our own?' Demelza must have been thinking of EasyJet.

Derek gave her another sniffy look. 'They have guides who speak English. They will stop you getting lost. You don't speak French.'

'Mais oui, I do,' Demelza preened.

'Shut it,' Jenna poked her. 'You know about five words. Go on Derek, this sounds fine.'

So Derek went on explaining. I was just amazed. He'd been to the tour company. He was able to buy everything – tickets, travel arrangements, hotel room, even Paris tours came as part of the package. It was all set out on paper.

'Cardboard tickets, wow.' I held one up.

Derek snatched it back. 'This is the newest ship; you will be very comfortable.'

All we had to do was turn up at the London station and everything would be done for us.

'You have luggage?' he asked.

'We don't have anything.' Demelza could see the chance of more shopping.

Derek explained that we could go to a store where Masterson had an account. He really shouldn't have said that. Demelza's eyes were rolling like an arcade game that had come up with the jackpot line.

'Now? We can go now?' Demelza jumped up.

Derek nodded.

'Hang on,' Jenna grabbed her. 'Not going anywhere until we get a few more details. How do we get away from this tour and go off looking for Miss Tregarthur?'

'The guide who comes with you is from England,' Derek was ready with more detail. 'I have told him you need to go and see someone, on your own. He wanted to know who it was, but I had been told not to tell anyone. You will be on your own.'

'How can we find Marie Curie?' I felt this was going to be difficult with no English speaking guide while we got lost in Paris. The page from Miss Tregarthur's book was the only information we had. It only had the name of the place she had worked.

Derek pulled out a map. 'This is the best I could find. It doesn't show exactly where Marie Curie lives or works, you'll have to ask.'

The map looked more like a tourist guide. Going over these plans in my head it felt as if an awful lot had been left out.

'How do we get back?' My first worry.

'The tour company will bring you.'

'But we might have Miss Tregarthur with us.' My second worry.

'I will ask Bill to get her a ticket.'

'She may not want to come.' My biggest worry.

If we took the crystal from her, why would she want to come with us? The only way I could see that happening was the use of violence, a lot of violence. I couldn't see that the tour company would help us to kidnap a struggling woman and drag her back to England.

Derek seemed flustered. 'You will have to contact me.'

'And you will do what, exactly?' Jenna said.

Derek's face was blank.

'And how do we contact you? Got your mobile number?' Jenna had picked up my next list of worries.

'Mobile what?' he asked and we just stared at him. 'No, you write to me.'

'What,' all three of us shouted.

'Yes, it is no problem.' Derek looked surprised.

'How many weeks is that going to take? For you to get the letter?' Jenna's turn to sniff.

'The post arrives from France the next day. You will get my reply often on the same day.' Derek thought that was obvious. He did have to give us a talk about the mail service which turned out to be incredibly fast, using boats and trains. Although we still didn't discover what Derek could actually achieve when we wrote to him.

'If we do this, it's bound to cost loads of money,' I said.

'Mr Masterson told me to give you this.' Derek very reluctantly handed over a leather pouch containing more of the white paper £5 notes and also some different money which Derek told us was French.

'What happens if we need more?' It looked like he'd given us quite a lot, but how far would that go? Kidnapping would be expensive.

'This is the name of a bank in Paris that you can go to.' Another reluctantly handed over piece of paper.

My mind was whizzing now. What had happened to make Masterson do all this? The white robed man on the moor said he would help, not spend a fortune. Masterson must be much more involved in all of this. We still hadn't figured out why Miss Tregarthur went to him in the first place. He wasn't mentioned in the pages from her book, not directly. It had only talked about men like him who had made loads of money with the new industries.

I suppose telling the world he was a spy might have worried him, but if he fled the country there was nothing we could do. There had to be something much more important and Derek had no idea what it could be.

The tour was going to leave in two days. That was enough time for Demelza to fill a suitcase from the store – a place called Harrods. Demelza had heard of it. Masterson's account didn't run to jewellery but Jenna did buy a watch.

'Clean pants,' Jenna gasped.

At least I did manage to get a few things that didn't actually make me smell like a camel.

Two days later we were standing outside a train station along with our luggage and a group of ten other people going on this trip to Paris. Bill, our guide, turned up beaming smiles and telling the sort of jokes that would get you arrested in more modern days. I had to stand between him and Jenna otherwise it would have been her that did get us arrested.

The train left on time, we met the boat, and that left on time. My sea sickness returned, something I'd had before, but the steam boat trip wasn't too long. Another train, French this time, but that left on time. Things leaving on time seemed normal. We knew everything was on time because of Jenna's watch and Bill, who kept telling us.

We arrived at the end of the line. Checking the map and the itinerary we'd been given this had to be the 'Gare du Nord' railway station. We climbed out with the rest of the people on the trip. Standing on the platform was confusing. Bill called us all together.

Porters were clamouring to carry our bags. Demelza was good at giving out orders and telling me to pay. Our group was bundled into a horse drawn bus. A double decker bus drawn by one exhausted looking horse. We trundled through the streets of Paris. The buildings were like those in London but more ornate. Everyone in our group pointed at the sights, laughed at French words and tried to repeat them with imitation accents. I think we joined in.

Demelza mostly sat with her nose in the air until, 'Look! Look!' she pointed. 'It's the Eiffel Tower.' And the bus nearly toppled over as we all leant out from one side.

There were more cars in Paris than London but they still weren't common – and breakdowns were a problem. Again there was a lot of shouting from the horse people with their carriages and carts. Not everyone was going to believe cars were helpful progress, not if their wages depended on horses.

After seeing the Eiffel Tower, Demelza stopped being snotty and was squirming in her seat. 'Where are the shops? The clothes?' she chirped in holiday mood.

It was true that the women on the streets looked a higher class than those in London, with fur things around their necks. Demelza said these were called 'stoles' and made me feel an idiot to think that meant stolen. Demelza used to know a lot about fashion and wanted to make sure she told us all about it.

The bus stopped at several places to drop off people on our trip, we weren't all staying at the same hotel. It depended how much you had paid. Derek made sure we three were together but not in the most expensive place.

'It's the same hotel Bill is staying at,' Derek had told us. 'You may need his help.'

We had two rooms next to each other on the fifth floor. Our hotel was a tall building squeezed in between a bank and some offices in a narrow cobbled street that led nowhere. Two glass panelled doors swung open leading into the entrance hall. They provided the only natural light in this dark and fusty place. A dried up plant in a chipped vase sat in one corner. I could almost smell the way the staff looked down at us, wanting to make sure we knew our place and not to expect too much comfort, but to keep quiet and behave nicely. Even Bill stopped telling jokes.

'Bill, where's the lift?' Demelza had the heaviest suitcase.

'Mademoiselle,' a lady behind a concierge desk cut across Bill. 'You can only use the lift before ten in the morning.'

She turned away.

Bill nodded in the background obviously anxious that we shouldn't argue.

'Why?' Demelza had a look of arguing.

'You walk up the stairs.' There was no more arguing because after handing us the keys the lady gave a huff and left the desk empty. We climbed the stairs.

Two rooms, the same size. Both with two beds. One room for me, one for the girls. The sort of furniture that made someone invent Ikea. The slope of the mattress suggested elephants had sat on my beds, a wardrobe with doors that swung open and stayed open, a chair unlikely to hold your weight, and notices in French with exclamation marks. Bill had told us there would be a meal at six, sharp.

Jenna came into my room and tried to bounce on one of the beds, it squeaked and rocked from side to side. A loud cough came from outside even though no one had climbed the stairs with us. We looked at each other and started laughing. After a few hysterical minutes there was a loud knock on the door.

Bill stood outside. 'She mustn't go into your room,' he said in a whisper. 'It is not allowed.'

We went down stairs at six. Food arrived later. About an hour later. Soup, bread and cheese. We'd eaten worse, but not much worse.

Bill had joined us. 'It is very French,' he said. He meant it was sophisticated, rather than his words being an insult.

He gave us a leaflet describing the plan for his tour the next day, how we would be met by a real French expert who would show us the sights. Demelza wanted to know all the details. Bill was keen to explain.

'Sorry Bill,' Jenna butted in. 'We have to go and see an old lady we know. Didn't Derek explain what we needed to do?'

Bill clearly thought we were missing the point, 'But you must see the Louvre, the Tower.'

Jenna shook her head.

'It won't be easy. You'll have to do it on your own.' Bill made that sound almost impossible.

Even with a bed broken in by heavyweights, I slept through the night. Jenna had to wake me, whispering in case the management showed up. Breakfast was bread and coffee. I think it came from the same loaf we'd had yesterday.

Leaving Bill with his other guests we walked out into the street and followed it down to the main road. This was as busy and noisy as London. We stood on the corner. Bill was right, this wasn't going to be easy.

'We have to ask.' Jenna looked around the street for someone helpful. I couldn't see anyone and I certainly couldn't speak French. Demelza knew a few words.

'Ask a policeman?' Demelza said, as though it was the obvious thing to do. I felt it was the most obvious way of getting us in jail. What were we going to ask: 'Have you seen a mad woman searching for a radioactive source?'

We wandered the streets for a while, looking for help. We started to notice the difference between here and London. Street lamps were more ornate, so were the horse carriages, there were more trees and flowers in this part of town and more people selling flowers. Men with top hats, curly hats, square hats, walking with women in long skirts carrying parasols but seeming to have no direction. Just walking and talking.

Jenna checked the map Derek had given us. 'He said we'd have to make for the river, it's called the Seine, don't know how you pronounce that. I'll ask.'

Jenna walked up to a couple and said something. They didn't stop, just walked on glowering at her. Jenna was puzzled. 'What did I do wrong?'

I was beginning to worry about us not fitting in. We'd been fine when we were with the tour group but now we stuck out again. Despite following Demelza's fashion advice we looked odd compared to the people on the Paris streets. It wouldn't be long before we drew enough attention to cause a problem. Anyone walking around here behaved as though they fitted in, lived here, the place wasn't full of tourists on their own.

'What's that?' Demelza pointed at a strange looking horse drawn cart. This one was being driven by a man in uniform with a cap.

'It says Poste.' Demelza pointed again at the cart. 'Poste et Telegraphes,' she read the French words. 'It's stopping at that building, might be a post office, couldn't we ask in there?'

We went in. Immediately I felt this was a mistake. The office was dark and brown everywhere – wood, walls, floor, dark brown and full of people who knew exactly what they were doing – and we didn't. The room went silent as we entered. Everyone turned to look at us. I wanted to run.

It was Demelza who strode up to a counter, placed the map on the desk, 'Excusee moi,' she said. 'Directions pour le Seine, si vous plait?'

I was impressed. The man behind the counter definitely wasn't. He drew himself up to his full height, puffed out his cheeks, 'LA … LA … LA Seine, she ees woman,' he almost shouted and muttered something about Les Eenglish which made the other customers laugh.

Demelza said something like 'whatever' but she smiled and the man relented, reluctantly, because he poured out a torrent of French and kept poking the map. This was not helpful. Demelza might have managed to get the question almost right but she had no idea what the post office man was spouting about. She turned to us and raised her eyebrows.

'Ello.' A woman tapped Jenna on the shoulder. 'Vous need 'elp?' She was an elderly looking woman and even though the day was quite warm she was dressed mostly in black with a heavy wrap of brown fur and a hat with a fur band.

Through a fractured conversation we explained about going to the river. Showing her our map.

'La Seine is very big, what you want?'

'Oh, for goodness sake just tell her,' Demelza went on. 'It's no use pretending this is some sort of secret.' She turned to the woman. 'Marie Curie. Alvin give me that piece of paper with her name.' She took the paper and showed it to the fur lady.

'Ah l'ecole, bonne, good, eet in Rue Vauequelin. Eer.' She stabbed her finger on our map before looking us up and down, sighed, 'You have monai?'

I nodded.

'It is easy. You call carriage, he take you.' The woman nearly dragged us outside. She waved to a row of horse drawn carriages and made us get in. The woman stayed on the pavement and gabbled out some directions which caused more shouting.

'He wants monai now.' The woman leant up to the window in the carriage. 'Is bad he want monai now, before you go.' She looked so unhappy that this had happened. 'I pay him.' She dived into her handbag and pulled out her purse. Jenna tried to get out and stop her but the woman was determined. 'You Eenglish must help us in war.' She pushed Jenna away.

Even I knew it was a few more years before the First World War, how did she know about it? Maybe it was more obvious to people in France. I wondered what would have happened if Miss Tregarthur had made her nuclear bomb. There wasn't any more time to argue or wonder because the carriage took off and we waved to the helpful lady.

Easy, I thought, just get a taxi. Now we were on our own private tour. The carriage bumped and banged its way across the cobbled streets. We passed open squares and green spaces, more men in hats – lots of striped trousers, nearly everyone in boots, women in long skirts and more hats.

We crossed the river.

'Do we want to get out before we get to this place?' I was trying to work out where we were from the map. The driver had started to take narrow side streets. I wondered if he was trying to get more money or perhaps was going to stop off and rob us. It was impossible to read anything with the lurching and bumping.

'Rue Tourne … something,' Jenna cried as we slowed down at a street sign. We had to slow in the narrow street with shops seeming to pour all their produce out into the road. Fruit, vegetables, café tables, places selling wine. A shop on a corner with rows and rows of boots.

'Not great shopping,' Demelza was developing a sneer in the less expensive streets. The posh men in hats and women in skirts were giving way to smocks and tunics. Might be less posh but I thought we'd fit in better here.

'Let me see the map.' Jenna tugged it from me. 'Thought so, this Rue Tourne-what's-it is close. OI! STOP,' she leant out of the window and shouted at the driver. Stop seemed to work and I had the impression that the driver was happy to get us out and return to the more expensive parts of town.

He was obviously going to ask for more money. Back home, I wouldn't have paid him but on the corner were a group of men in uniforms I hadn't any idea what they were. Could be police, could be anything and I didn't want to be answering a load of questions. Jenna had the purse in her bag and I nodded towards it. We paid. The man gave us a smirk so I guessed he wasn't expecting it and we probably paid too much. And we were alone again. The uniformed men had wandered off. The streets were strangely silent here, tall stone buildings looming over us. The shops had all closed. In the distance I could see a café with tables and chairs outside.

'Lunchtime,' muttered Demelza, our supposed French expert. 'Everything stops for lunch.' She looked up at a sign. 'It says Ecole something up there, Rue Vauquelin over there. That's where the lady from the post office said we had to go. The Ecole something, she told us. That's where Marie Curie works.'

'It's an ordinary street,' I said, wondering if an ordinary street was the sort of place you did research into radiation?

'Don't suppose they knew what it was when they discovered it,' Jenna said.

'What … what the?' Demelza was staring up another street at a strange looking man selling things. His rounded hat, his felt jacket, his moustache, his shoes like slippers and all of that might have been quite ordinary but … 'He's selling lampshades.' And he was. They were piled in a large basket attached to his back.

As he walked past us he waved one shade in our direction shouting something like 'marching about jours' but probably I was way off the mark. Demelza didn't know either and started to laugh. That wasn't a great idea and we had to push off quickly. Luckily all his lampshades made it difficult for him to chase us.

Crossing over to the Rue Vauquelin we were nearly knocked over by two people on bicycles. We hadn't seen many bicycles and I guess they were uncomfortable on the cobbles. These two were in a hurry, probably late for their lunch.

'It's them,' Jenna was holding up the page from Miss Tregarthur's book. 'Marie and Pierre Curie. You can tell by his beard and her – she's actually wearing a puffed up shirt, like in the picture …'

'A bouffant blouse,' Demelza chipped in with the fashion correction.

'Still doesn't look like the sort of thing you'd wear in a laboratory,' Jenna didn't like being corrected by Demelza.

But it wasn't their clothes or their bicycles that made me stiffen against the wall and pull the two girls back with me. Further down the street another figure emerged from the shadows and walked off in the direction the Curies had come from. I could recognise that figure anywhere. The figure of Miss Alice Tregarthur.

We watched her walk on, while we stayed flattened against the wall as she looked around before darting through a doorway.

'What do we do now?' I said, the sight of that woman made me shiver.

-16-

COFFEE

'Simple,' Demelza turned to me. 'We go down there, grab the crystal and head home.'

I wasn't sure I had any argument with that. Jenna stayed silent.

'If we get the crystal, she'll follow us, we all go to that old man with the white robe on the moor, deliver her and it's all over,' I said, to the still silent Jenna.

'If we go to that café,' Jenna pointed across the road. 'Any chance you could get us a coffee or whatever?' She said to Demelza.

'Use my French?' Demelza sounded surprised.

'Yep,' Jenna said, although I didn't know if she really liked coffee. We still went over to the café. Miss Tregarthur didn't reappear. There wasn't much to see on the street where the Curies worked. I wondered if we should be going after her, see exactly where she went. Maybe she would finish what she had to do and leave. I didn't want that to happen without us knowing.

We sat outside the café on heavy iron seats, outside in tree shaded Paris, the smell of food, lunch was ending although the customers were taking their time. It did almost feel like a holiday. I missed our school trip to France. Missed that and nearly everything else.

'I could get used to this,' I said, leaning back.

Jenna moved her chair and sat looking down the street – the Rue Vauquelin. A perfect view, not a view obscured by parked cars – no parking problem in this year – only an old cart and a couple of rusting broken bicycles. Probably the cobbles had been too bumpy for their riders. Why had Jenna made us sit here? Why were we waiting out here?

'Café?' Demelza asked the shuffling bored waiter who appeared after a long wait and who whipped off a few phrases of French and a shrug. His words didn't make sense to Demelza and certainly not to me. He was about to turn away and didn't appear particularly bothered if he had taken our order or not.

I stood up in front of him, blocking his way. 'Three coffees, mate.' I held up three fingers to make my point. He curled his lip at me so I prodded him in the chest. 'Ok?' That made sense. I saw an elderly lady come out of the restaurant and call to him, she swiped him around the head and gave him a torrent of words, the meaning all too clear, we got the coffee – no milk. It was hard earned coffee and I was going to drink it, no matter what, and anyway nothing was happening in the Rue what's-it.

'What next?' I wanted some sugar, which hadn't arrived on the tables. 'What's your idea Jen?'

Jenna was still quiet but leant forward. 'Miss Tregarthur has come here to get that crystal to work. She must have gone into the Curies' laboratory. She needs this stronger radiation. If it doesn't work, she's stuck.'

'She did get the tunnel to bring her here,' Demelza said.

'It didn't get her home, it didn't get her to the time she wanted.' Jenna poked the table with her finger stressing each word, 'We don't know what she had planned next.'

'Does that matter? If we get her back to that old man he said he'd get us home.' I wanted to get on with this, whatever we were going to do.

'Yes, he said that.' Jenna paused. 'But he's part of the family. Do we trust him? I don't know. He wants Alice Tregarthur back, so he said, but how do we know he'll keep his promise after that?'

'So what do we do?' Demelza sounded cross that we hadn't done what she'd suggested and weren't trying to take the crystal from Miss Tregarthur. She took a swig of the coffee, which made her choke. It wasn't coffee like we knew it.

'First we need to find out if she can make the crystal work again with whatever she is doing at the laboratory,' Jenna pointed down the road. 'If it works and then we take it from her we might be able to get the tunnel to work for us. Otherwise we just have to rely on that man.'

'How do we find out if she succeeds?' I asked. 'If she does we might miss her. She could run off without us taking the crystal from her.'

'She'll head to the moor anyway,' Jenna said. 'We just have to get there before her.'

Should we have bothered going after her at all? Had we been sent on this wild chase by the man on the moor – one of Miss T's relatives? Surely we needed to do more than wait. There was no sign of anything happening further down the street.

Jenna took the scarf she had bought in London, pulled it over her head and tied it under her chin. Along with the new clothes it was quite a good disguise.

'You two stay here while I take a look.' Before we could disagree Jenna strode off towards the laboratories, if that was what they were.

'Do you believe that Jenna's right?' Demelza said, after Jenna had left and she moved her chair a little closer. 'What do you think, Alvin?' and she laid her hand on mine.

'More coffee,' I said, jumping back while Demelza laughed at me.

'Not drinking anymore of that stuff, let's try something else,' Demelza turned towards the waiter who was lurking near the restaurant door. 'Garcon,' she cried and the boy came over. 'Avez vous la glace?' Demelza's French had suddenly improved – I somehow wished I'd had a little more time in school.

'Oui,' the waiter seemed quite astonished. 'Quelle sorte?'

'Vanille,' Demelza smiled and we got vanilla ice cream.

'Didn't know any other flavours,' Demelza laughed with lukewarm ice-cream melting around her mouth. That made me smile at the wrong time because Jenna reappeared.

'You two having a good time,' Jen muttered.

'See anything?' I asked quickly as Jenna sat down and took my ice-cream for herself.

'Miss Tregarthur was in the laboratory. I don't believe it was locked. It's a primitive sort of place.'

'How did you manage to see?' I asked.

'There's a window at the side, easy to look in and Miss T didn't notice. She was too busy.'

'Doing what?' Demelza had just dribbled a lump of ice-cream onto her chest and was frantically looking for something to wipe it off. There weren't any napkins, but another smile brought the waiter with a cloth. He seemed to have melted, like the ice-cream.

'She was standing at a glass cabinet,' Jenna said. 'I saw her take the crystal thing out of her bag and ...'

'What happened?' I leant forward.

'There was a space at the back with a pile of beakers and other glass. She put the crystal under them and left it there. Then she got out. I had to run and hide behind that cart.' She pointed down the road again.

'We didn't see her leave,' I said.

'Probably having too good a time,' Jenna barked. 'If you'd been watching you would have seen her come back up the street and go into one of the houses. She must be staying there, there's sign outside which says 'chambres' which I think means rooms?' Jenna looked to Demelza who nodded.

'The cabinet has to be where the radium is kept and she's left the crystal to get more radiation – bit like we did on the moor.' Jenna finished my ice-cream. 'We just have to work out how long she is going to leave it there.'

I didn't want to argue with Jen, especially with Demelza around. But this sounded too difficult. Unless we watched the laboratories all the time Miss Tregarthur could easily slip away if the crystal started working again.

'We need to find a place to stay around here.' Jenna poked Demelza. 'How about asking your nice waiter boy?'

The waiter was no use, but the woman, who was his mother, found someone who spoke English and she was happy to offer us a room, for money, one bed. So we camped out there. A small window gave a view down the Rue Vauquelin. We tried to keep watch but nothing happened and the day was ending.

'She's going to leave it there overnight, I'm sure,' I said, without confidence, before making for the bed and being pushed on to the floor by the two girls. I thought Jenna was making me pay for the ice cream – and perhaps the laughter she had heard.

Next day, Saturday, was still quiet on the road. The waiter had become more friendly – with Demelza – which at least let me off the hook as she flirted with him and she managed to get tea with milk and some breakfast. Jenna put her scarf back on and went to look at the laboratory.

'The crystal is still there,' Jenna said, when she returned.

'You went into the laboratory?' I wondered if that was safe.

'No, I just looked through the window again.'

'You could see enough?' I asked.

'Probably.' Jenna turned to Demelza. 'What's on the menu?'

'There isn't a menu.' Demelza loved knowing more than we did. 'You go into the kitchen and point at whatever you want.'

We ate and drank through the day, again sitting outside. Other people came and went. Demelza told me the food smelt of garlic, and drains. I quite liked the food, not the drains. The weather stayed warm. Perhaps we might have to stay here forever.

We didn't see the Curies again. They must have left for the weekend, maybe a cycling trip. It seemed strange there was no security at this place, with the radiation.

We saw Miss Tregarthur go down the road several times and disappear into the laboratory. What was she doing? There was no way to tell. Each time she came back I wondered if she had the crystal with her. There could easily be a back way out of the place she was staying, we'd have no idea if she left.

Jenna went again. 'I tried to get in, but the laboratory is actually locked, Miss Tregarthur must have got a key from somewhere.'

'Under a brick?' I asked.

'I looked, not stupid,' Jenna huffed.

'No light coming from the crystal?' I didn't want Jenna to get cross.

'Not that I could see.' Jenna was watching Demelza fluttering her eyes at the waiter while his mother glared.

Jenna went on, 'I'd guess Miss Tregarthur has picked the weekend, while the Curies are away. That means she'll take the crystal tomorrow or maybe even early Monday before they get to work.'

We watched and waited. Miss Tregarthur went to the laboratory on Sunday morning. We saw her go down the road rather slowly. She came back later and almost staggered on the pavement outside the house where she must have been staying. She didn't come out again.

On Monday morning still nothing happened. Miss Tregarthur didn't appear. Jenna said we should all go to the house advertising 'chambres'.

-17-

Malade

The dusty green wood-panelled door stood open, open for business, not a hotel but something smaller, just rooms. Where had Miss Tregarthur eaten her meals, I wondered? There was a strong smell about the place.

Demelza sniffed. 'Cabbage? Boiled cabbage?' she spoke in a whisper because this was a place that made you want to whisper, old, musty and dark even in the summer light. We heard shuffling and a woman appeared. Shabbily dressed but her hair in the most amazing pink rollers.

'Hello?' she said as a question without us having told her anything. 'You are English?'

'You speak English?' Jenna said, with surprise.

'Oui, yes, of course, I am an English landlady.' She had stopped in the hall and the way she stood made it clear we weren't to go any further.

'Explains the cabbage smell, very English,' Demelza whispered in my ear.

'We have another English woman staying here.' She fingered her hair as she spoke and let her words hang in the air waiting to see what we would say.

We didn't look like guests and she could simply guess why we had come, but anything to do with Miss Tregarthur worried me, this lady worried me.

'Can we see her?' Jenna said.

'You are?' the woman snapped.

'Alvin.' Jenna pointed at me. 'Alvin is her nephew.'

Where did that come from? I knew Jenna was fast on her thinking feet, but Miss Tregarthur a relative? That … I thought a bit more. The white robed man, he knew my name. Other coincidences I had tried to forget. Was there truth in Jenna's words?

'Alvin.' Jenna poked me, I'd been miles away.

'Yes … my aunt. Is she in?' I said.

Her half smile told me the English landlady didn't believe my aunt story. She opened a desk drawer.

'Oh, she must be here, her key is not here. I thought she'd gone out.' Not finding the key seemed to surprise her. 'She always leaves her key when she goes out, I don't think … she must be in her room,' she said, almost to herself before turning to us: 'Stay here.' She pointed to the ground. 'Right here.' And she disappeared behind a curtain. We heard her footsteps on the stairs.

'Hope aunty is there,' Demelza smirked.

We waited in silence, fixed to the spot as we had been told. The dingy musty hallway with its smell of cabbage made me uneasy. Were there more people here? Were we in danger and not just from Miss Tregarthur?

The silence broke with the woman's scream: 'MALADE. MALADE.'

Jenna looked at me and we all rushed up the stairs. The lady with the hair rollers stood at the half open door to one of the bedrooms. Her hands on her head and a desperate look on her face as she muttered, 'Malade,' over and over again before collapsing onto a chair on the landing, still muttering and holding out her hand in a not very convincing way to stop us going into the bedroom.

Jenna pushed her aside and we went in. It was quite difficult to see what was going on in the room. Everywhere in this place was dark. Jenna pulled back some ancient curtains and light flooded in through the tall windows. The room was barely furnished – a bed, chair, few other things – and, slipping from the bed on to the floor, Miss Tregarthur. She looked up at us with sunken eyes.

'You.' She raised a pointed finger before her hand flopped to the floor. She tried to move. The effort was too great and she slumped back, groaning. Around her a terrible sight of blood and vomit.

The landlady had gone to pieces, sitting on her chair, rocking back and forth, babbling in a mixture of French and English: 'Malade, what do I do, aide mois, what must I do?'

Strange that none of us felt sympathy for her or the person on the floor.

'Where's the crystal?' Jenna prodded Miss Tregarthur with her toe, 'Where?'

Miss Tregarthur didn't manage an answer but half raised her hand again as though pointing somewhere.

'Is it at the lab?' Jenna prodded her again. That made the landlady moan even louder but Miss Tregarthur gave a weak nod.

'You two clean her up, get her downstairs.' Jenna started ordering us. 'I'll get the crystal and meet you back here. I need to hurry and hope Marie Curie isn't there.'

'Then what?' Demelza obviously didn't like the idea of cleaning up the mess.

'Then we take her to the tour hotel and see if that guide man can help.' Jenna made it sound possible. 'Stick with the aunty story,' Jenna whispered to me before she turned and started to leave.

'Hang on,' I said. 'I don't know anything about it but this illness she has, vomiting blood. Has the crystal caused it? Is it dangerous? Is she going to die? Can we catch it?'

Miss Tregarthur muttered something from the floor.

'What?' I asked her.

She croaked and tried again, 'Radiation.'

'Radiation?' Demelza said, and we looked at her.

Jenna nodded. 'I thought it had to be that.'

'From the crystal?' I put a hand out to stop Jenna leaving. 'It won't be safe. Don't you need to do something to make it safe?'

'Lead, put it in something made of lead.' Demelza might be the most hateable person on the planet but she did seem to know stuff. Not everyone was as ignorant as me.

'I'll see if there's anything in the lab.' Jenna pulled away from me and started to leave.

'Wait,' I called her back. 'The key.' On a shelf by the bed were two keys, one with a tag and the hotel name, the other had to be the key to the laboratory. I handed it to Jenna.

Cleaning up Miss Tregarthur wasn't a job I wanted to do. Neither was Demelza a competent medical aid.

'Is she going to die?' The landlady had returned to the doorway.

Weird that this woman should be asking us, what did she think we were, some sort of medical team? I stared at her without speaking.

'You'll take her away?' She'd heard Jenna's words.

'Yes,' I answered. It was obvious that the woman's distress was more about the difficulty this would cause her than the health of Miss Tregarthur. Made me wonder what an English landlady was doing here – perhaps she was running from something.

'You promise to take her away?'

I nodded. That promise set the landlady to work on Miss Tregarthur – demanding help from us to get water and towels from the kitchen. It wasn't long before she'd stripped off the blood stained clothes and found a clean smock from somewhere. Miss Tregarthur didn't seem to have the strength to resist.

Once the landlady had set to work we searched the room. There wasn't much to find.

Demelza pulled out a drawer. 'The rest of her book,' she called out. 'What do we do with it?'

'In the bin … no.' I realised that anyone finding it would be reading about their future. That might not be a good idea. 'Stick it in her bag and we'll burn it later.'

We ended up with a small bag of her possessions. Odd that I didn't find the iron bar she had used to hit her crystal at the Hanging Stones.

In the end Miss Tregarthur still looked sick but at least cleaner.

'Get her downstairs,' the landlady ordered. 'Keep the towel around her in case she's sick again.'

So, with a small amount of help from Demelza, I lifted and dragged Miss Tregarthur down the narrow stairs and dumped her on a chair in the hall with towels all around her.

Then Jenna appeared carrying a small metal box. 'Got it,' she said.

'Did you look at it?' I wanted to know if the radiation might have made any difference to the crystal.

'Not really, have to check it later,' Jenna said, but giving me a slight wary glance. 'I found a padlock and key with it.' She pointed at a small lock holding a clasp on the box. Not something that wouldn't break easily but I suppose it would stop anyone taking a quick look, the anyone being Demelza.

I tapped the box. 'Is it lead?' It was the size of something you'd use to keep biscuits in, heavier but not thick metal.

'I hope so.' Jenna turned to the landlady. 'How do we get a cab – I mean carriage?'

The woman might be an English landlady but she was well organised in this country. She went to the front door and whistled, expertly, with two fingers in her mouth. A high pitched whistle. We didn't have to wait long before a young boy, dressed for street life rather than anything else, turned up and our landlady gave out a string of French before the lad took off again.

'What did you tell him?' I was still suspicious.

'To get a carriage to take you wherever you need to go.' I caught the catch in the woman's voice. This was moving into the sort of things I knew about from my home. She wanted us gone and she didn't want to see us again. Might just be that the carriage took us somewhere we didn't want to go. Somewhere we couldn't ever come back from.

'Where in England are you from?' I asked and she just flicked her head, not prepared to give me an answer.

Ok, I had picked up tips, the bad sort, from my dad but this trip had given me more confidence to use them. I also can whistle, so I went out onto the road and whistled. Another boy soon turned up.

The landlady moved away with her eyes blazing. Was she done? I worried that she might try something else.

I turned to Demelza. 'Any idea of the word for carriage?'

'Don't think it's voiture 'cos that's a car.' Demelza scratched her head. 'It might be something like chariot – try chariot.'

We did try. We probably didn't make any sense. Jenna tried to explain to the boy by waving her arms like a horse driver. The boy nodded and ran off.

'Stay out on the street,' I said to Jenna and Demelza. 'Any trouble and you run for it.'

'And you?' Jenna smiled.

'I'll be the one causing the trouble.' I tried to sound brave but it was just pretence.

The landlady returned and she wasn't alone, two men stood behind her. 'Where are the girls?'

'Back off,' I said. 'The girls will run for it if they have to and you'll be left with her.' I pointed at Miss Tregarthur who was slipping slowly from her chair, not seeming to notice. 'You'll be left with her and the mess.' I turned back. 'And there might be people in England who would be interested in an English landlady hiding here in this part of Paris.'

I could feel the sweat trickling down my neck. I made myself think of all the other terrible things that we'd managed to avoid. I would be brave. I'd done it before.

The landlady gave me the sourest of looks before turning to the men and waving them away. Two carriages turned up and their drivers argued.

The argument started to bring other people on to the street. One was the guy selling lampshades. I'd seen him a couple of times. He was different. He certainly behaved differently as he brought out his own whistle and gave several loud blasts. It fell into place. This street seller had probably been watching the landlady. Was he calling the police? If it wasn't them, it could be someone worse.

I suppose anywhere Miss Tregarthur had contacts was likely to be less than legal. The landlady might want her taken away if she was sick, if she looked like dying, but that might mean something else was going on. The landlady had been quick to find two men to back her up – two men who disappeared when Mr Lampshade started whistling.

The landlady's pink rollers were starting to come loose as she became more agitated. She started shouting that she was owed money.

'No way.' Jenna came inside and we heaved Miss Tregarthur into the second carriage, I gave the boy, the one I'd called, several coins. His eyes widened and he ran off with the other boy chasing after him.

'Move it,' I called to our driver. It wasn't French but he grasped what was needed. We could already hear running feet – people had been called by the lampshade man. I didn't want to find out who they were.

Behind us the landlady slammed her front door and both carriage drivers took off at speed. They didn't want to stay around to find out who was coming either. Our man turned into narrow streets away from the main roads. A little later he stopped and shouted something down to us.

'He must want to know where we are going.' Jenna scrabbled in her bag and drew out the itinerary for our tour. She got out and pointed at the name of our hotel. He wanted money and he got it, no arguing from us, we wanted to get there. We were off again.

We'd paid for the hotel so I hoped the rooms would still be free. But would we be able to get Miss Tregarthur through the door? She looked unconscious to me, although still giving out the occasional groan and a nasty wheezing noise. Difficult to know how much of her illness could be put on, this was a woman we knew we couldn't trust.

The carriage journey took all morning as we had to slow in the Paris traffic. We were lucky to arrive at the hotel during the Parisian lunchtime. The hotel appeared deserted, with its doors closed. Miss Tregarthur was a dead weight. At least she hadn't vomited again. Demelza refused to go near her.

'Chuck her over your shoulder.' Jenna climbed down from the carriage. 'I'll check to see if there's anyone around.' She paid the driver and walked away to the hotel glass doors. 'Wait until I come back,' she called and disappeared inside.

I heaved Miss Tregarthur out, staggered to the side of the road with her still moaning and I leant against the wall, waiting.

Jenna came out almost immediately. 'Seems quiet, come on,' and I followed her in.

'Oi! Monsieur, what you do?' A man popped up from behind the concierge desk.

Oh, we're just bringing in a murderous sick woman with radiation sickness. Might have been a good answer, but none of us had the words or the nerve to say that in any language.

'I get Bill,' the man shouted. 'You stay. Put her there.' He pointed to the chairs by the door and went behind a curtain.

We dumped Miss Tregarthur on to one of them, she retched again. I stuffed a towel over her face. 'Come on Aunty,' I said, and not in a nice way. This woman had done too much harm for me to care. I still worried whether radiation sickness was catching.

'Stick to the aunt story,' Jenna repeated, as we heard someone coming down the stairs.

-18-

REPATRIATION

Bill the tour guide arrived, a bit dishevelled. This was his rest time, the only time he had when people on the tour were taken away by local guides.

'Your aunt, you say?'

'She's not well,' I said.

'Oh, really? I would never have guessed.' Bill stared at our sick Miss Tregarthur, half sliding from a chair and seeming to be fast asleep or unconscious, blood still showing on the towels we had kept around her. Blood still at the corners of her mouth. 'What do you want me to do about it?'

'Did Derek say we might need to get her home?' I had a mind to say something stupid, like take her up the Eiffel Tower, but Bill wasn't a person ready for that.

'He didn't say she'd be ...' Bill lowered his voice to a whisper, 'nearly dead.'

Miss Tregarthur decided to let out a moan. Again it made me wonder how ill she really was.

'Actually,' Bill remembered something. 'It won't be a problem. I know someone who takes visitors to Lourdes.' He checked to see if I understood. 'You know the place where the miracles happened. They get thousands of visitors.'

'Lots of them nearly dead?' I asked.

I could see Bill was going to say yes, but he checked himself. 'Many of them are not well. Mr Jackson, a man I know, sorts out their travel. He's staying at the Majestic. I'll send him a note and ask him to come here.'

Bill was pleased. Solving problems was his job. He was very pleased to have come up with a solution for Miss Tregarthur. Too much of a coincidence for me.

'It will cost quite a lot,' Bill added. 'Is that a problem?'

That explained the coincidence, a lot of coincidences involved money.

'No problem,' Jenna said, stopping me from asking questions about the cost. 'When can we get away?'

'I suppose that depends on the cost.' Bill was already leaning on the desk writing his note. When he finished he gave it to the French concierge who went outside, whistled and another boy took the note and ran off.

'Oh.' Bill turned to us again with a look of panic. 'Can't leave her here. Can you get her up to one of your rooms?'

'How?' I asked.

'In the lift,' Bill said something in French to the concierge, there was arguing.

'Can't use the lift, it's after 10,' Jenna said, with a slight smile.

After we'd paid extra, it meant dragging Miss Tregarthur to the lift. It was operated by ropes and pulleys. I helped to haul the cage up to our floor. I could see why they didn't want people using the lift, it took ages and a lot of pulling.

'I'll send Mr Jackson up to you when he …' Bill stopped. A strange looking man with an enormous beard came into the hotel lobby. Whatever the mail system might be, this note sending seemed faster than phoning. I supposed that Bill had written something about money.

'It will cost,' Mr Jackson's first words to me as we went up to my room.

'It will cost, quite a lot,' he said, after seeing her.

Overall, this would take the rest of the money Derek had given us – money to Mr Jackson, some more to Bill, more to the hotel, the boy outside, pretty much anyone we met was hoping we'd give them something. We still had enough and didn't need to go to the bank. Made me realise again how much Masterson must have wanted this problem to go away.

Mr Jackson could get us on a train in the morning, then to catch the boat and another train to London. 'After that you are on your own.' Then he took my arm, guided me to the doorway and said in a hushed voice, 'Let me know if she doesn't survive the night.'

I thought that would be all he had to say, it wasn't, he went on: 'Won't be a problem if she's dead, still get you there but …' he stopped.

'It'll cost more?' I said it for him. He nodded and left with a pile of our money.

After he'd left Jenna reminded me that we had to send a letter to Derek telling him we were going to need more help.

'How do we know what time the train will arrive?' It still felt so strange to write a letter which should get to Derek before we arrived tomorrow.

Jenna went down to the hotel desk, wrote the note and had it taken off to the post. 'Hope Derek can work it out,' she said, after climbing the stairs again, no lift this time. 'If he doesn't turn up I suppose we can just leave her on the train.'

'We could hang a note around her neck with Masterson's

name on it.' I thought that was quite a good idea even if Derek had other suggestions.

Miss Tregarthur lay on the empty bed in my room.

'I'm not staying all night with her on my own,' I told the other two.

Demelza offered to do it. I didn't know why she offered. Jenna and I listened several times at their door during the night. Demelza snored. Miss Tregarthur moaned. Jenna and I got away with sharing. I suppose the management had given up on us.

'Did you look at the crystal?' I asked when we were alone. 'Any change?'

'Maybe,' Jenna said, 'I didn't look at properly, there wasn't time. I found the metal box and chucked the crystal into it quickly,' Jenna said.

'Should we check it now?' I pointed at the box on the floor.

'Do you want to get killed?' Jenna murmured. 'Just go to sleep will you.'

Early in the morning Bill knocked on our two doors and told us to bring her down. The lift was less effort going down. Mr Jackson wasn't there but he had sent his Lourdes team. Three men lifted Miss Tregarthur into a carriage – a sort of horse drawn ambulance. Riding on top, there was room to take us all.

Bill waved as we left. He was very pleased to see us go. I think his smile meant he had an arrangement with the Jackson man. Medical repatriation obviously could make good money.

We arrived at Waterloo Station the next afternoon. The trip had gone easily, more of Mr Jackson's team helping to get

Miss Tregarthur on and off the boat. No wonder it had been expensive. This time the sea was quite calm so Miss Tregarthur was the only sick one of us.

Waterloo – above me it could have been a railway station in my own time, look down and the place was full of horses and carriages, right on the platform. This next part depended on Derek. Did he get our letter? Did that really work, a one-day letter to Derek and we were expecting him to be at the station?

If he wasn't here, we would have to abandon her. Miss Tregarthur seemed worse. She had vomited more blood – luckily we'd taken a load of towels and sheets from the hotel. I decided they were included in the cost of this trip. It hadn't kept her completely clean. If we took her on to the platform, everyone would notice. Leaving her on the train and disappearing could well be the best option.

Jenna climbed out of our compartment. 'I'll see if anyone has come for us.'

Just as she did a man walked along the platform shouting, 'Miss Tregarthur group, Miss Tregarthur group.' Over and over. He walked right past us.

Jenna had to run after him. 'Stop, come back.'

The man turned and saw me leaning out of the train door. He turned and shouted. Derek and two more men appeared with a sort of trolley, a flat board and four huge wheels. Fine for Miss Tregarthur, although it looked like the sort of thing you might use to make a market stall. We wouldn't get much for her if we tried.

'Are we going to Masterson's house?' Jenna asked Derek.

'SHHH,' he cried. 'Don't use that name. You're off on the next train. It's a couple of platforms away.'

That made sense. Masterson didn't want to see us or have any contact with us. He would help, provided we kept her away from London, took her back to the moor if we could – unless she died. I had no idea what we would do if that happened. Arranging funerals wasn't one of my skills. Although we'd had several deaths since we had left on that first moorland hike.

We pushed the cart. Derek ran off to a large black carriage which had stopped near the station entrance. The windows were covered with a curtain. Derek lent in saying something, nodded and afterwards he returned to us.

'You three stay here,' he ordered before getting the men to wheel Miss Tregarthur towards the carriage. A face appeared, leant out, and then disappeared quickly before the carriage drove off. It had to have been Masterson making sure we had brought the right person.

I wondered what he would do now. He had been about to leave the country. But wasn't that just in case Miss Tregarthur returned and exposed him as a spy? Was there any risk now? If he stayed, he still had the copies of Miss Tregarthur's pages about weapons of war – even the nuclear bomb. We couldn't do anything about that, we were about to join another train.

Derek had hired another complete compartment for us, like the one we had used from Paris. Again, we laid Miss Tregarthur out on the seats on one side. She gave several weak moans as we lowered her down. Most of the time her eyes were shut. Just once they flicked open. I wasn't fooled. She was still holding on; I was sure this wasn't over.

'Is there a machine for water or coke or something,' Demelza moaned, before we got in. 'I'm parched.'

Derek laughed at her. 'You want water?' he said. 'Wouldn't

drink the water here. And you can't drink coke – just put it on the fire. The journey must have muddled your mind.'

Demelza sniffed at him. A woman did come along the platform pushing a huge metal urn and selling tea. I wasn't a great tea drinker, even less after trying her thick dark brew without milk and the sugar didn't help. She had given us real cups and explained that they would be collected at the next station. I thought that was a better idea than dropping paper cups on the floor, modern things weren't always an improvement.

The cart men disappeared. We took our places on the seat opposite our patient. Derek handed me a letter. 'Don't expect we'll see you again,' he said, as a warning.

A few minutes later the train left with a great amount of hissing of steam. I read the letter before passing it to Jenna:

"This train will take you to Exeter. Get straight on the next train towards the moor. I have someone watching you, they will help with the transfer. DO NOT stop. DO NOT come back. DO NOT contact me again."

The envelope contained several more white five pound notes.

'That's clear enough,' Jenna half laughed. 'I wonder what Masterson will do now.' Jenna echoed the thoughts I'd had on the platform. 'Perhaps we should have done more – told someone that he might be on the other side in the war.'

'It's a few more years before the war starts.' Demelza had grabbed the letter. 'If you'd ever been at our school you'd have heard there were lots of people who sympathised with the Germans before the First World War.'

I didn't argue although I'm not convinced Demelza's school attendance was that great. I did think that Masterson might have been doing more than sympathising, even if he wasn't building a nuclear bomb – or was he?

Jenna was silent for a while. Then she spoke, seeming to choose each word carefully: 'If we get back to our own time, if … if it's the same as before … then … well then he can't have done anything? Can he?'

That led me to a lot of worrying. About how history might change with all this time travel.

'What do we do if it's all different?' I said later.

Neither Jenna nor Demelza had an answer to that. The only person who might have known the answer was in a coma and taking up three seats opposite. Probably in a coma, maybe.

'Pies, pies,' came a shout from along the narrow corridor outside our compartment. A man in a tweed coat, flat cap, baggy trousers and a white apron knocked on our door and peered in.

'Blimey,' he said in the sort of accent that really did make us laugh because it sounded like something off an old TV show, old London. 'Whot yerr done to 'er,' and he pointed at Miss Tregarthur, whose drawn face and sunken eyes made her look like a corpse.

'Can we buy some pies?' Demelza broke in and I was glad she did. We didn't want to get involved in a conversation about radiation sickness.

The man sold them to us in the train corridor. 'Ain't goin' in there.'

We stayed in the corridor to eat our pies, Miss Tregarthur was a sight to make anyone lose their appetite.

'Chewy,' Jenna said, pulling a lump of gristle out of her mouth and chucking it through the train window – we had opened them again after the tunnels leaving London.

'Do we give her something?' Demelza asked.

We had tried to give her some tea but she retched and it came back up. I wondered how long she could last without food or drink.

There was a toilet on the train. Jenna went and filled her empty tea cup from a tap. 'It said not for drinking, but it's the best we've got,' she said, tilting Miss Tregarthur's head forward and pouring a few dribbles of water into her mouth. That stayed down so Jenna gave her a bit more.

The train hooted to warn of another tunnel and I rushed to close the windows. Again, I wondered if I saw Miss Tregarthur move.

The train rumbled on and on. We stopped at a station. Another woman on the platform took our dirty cups and offered to sell us more tea, it didn't look any better. More hooting and the train pulled out. The same thing happened at every station.

I watched the countryside pass by, keeping an eye on our patient.

'Her hair's falling out,' Demelza's lip curled. She was right, Miss Tregarthur's wild straw-like hair was coming out in clumps.

'That happens with radiation,' Demelza said, with confidence.

'We all know that,' Jenna said.

'Eh?' I had no idea.

'Saw it with my nan,' Demelza went on: 'They gave her radiation for cancer and her hair all fell out, she had to wear a wig until it grew again.'

'Did she survive?' I asked. This might give a clue to whether we might expect Miss Tregarthur to recover.

'For a while,' Demelza replied. 'Not long though, she's dead now.' And did Demelza give a sob? I found it difficult to imagine her as being the sort of person who would care for anyone other than herself. At least the flirting had stopped.

Eventually I drifted off to sleep, waking at each tunnel and each time we stopped. We did what Derek ordered. Two more men helped move Miss Tregarthur on to the next train heading for the grey moorland town. Getting another compartment to ourselves cost one of the five pound notes. I knew we'd been cheated but the man said he had no change and the train was about to leave. It didn't really matter to us – if we got home I didn't think we could use these old notes – probably wrong about that, maybe they would be valuable antiques.

I hoped this was to be our last train journey. Finding the compartment stuffy, I stretched and walked the corridor, getting back to a worried looking Jenna.

'What do we do at the end of this journey?' Jenna had dark rings around her eyes and her face was creased with tiredness. 'It's going to be dark before we arrive.' We'd been travelling for two days. 'We can't take her up to the moor in the dark.'

'Not sure how we take her up to the moor even when it's daylight,' I said and Jenna nodded.

'Have to stay in that inn,' Demelza gave her smirky smile. 'The inn we stayed at before.'

I knew what she meant – the inn where she'd annoyed Jenna and worried me with her pouting and eyelid batting.

'You get the bed with her.' Jenna pointed at Miss Tregarthur.

'Yuck,' Demelza squirmed. 'No way I'm sharing a bed.'

'How do we get her to the inn? Do we carry her? Won't that start people asking questions?' I said.

'She's your sick aunt and we're taking her home.' Jenna had this sorted out. 'And I did see wheelchairs at the last station, people were being pushed around. We may find one at the next place.'

'Can't push her all the way up to the moor,' I said.

'No,' Jenna went on: 'But we can get a horse and cart or something.'

I sat thinking about this for the rest of the journey. Miss Tregarthur on a cart being bumped along. But even that wouldn't get us out on to the moor. There were no roads out in the wilds, just a few sheep tracks.

In a previous time when we'd been escaping from being burnt alive, we had thrown Zach and Demelza over a horse and tied them on. Was that what we'd have to do with Miss Tregarthur? I didn't like the idea of trying to carry her all the way. I still wasn't entirely convinced that she was as sick as she appeared.

'Should we check the …' I stopped as Jenna raised her finger to her lips and shook her head. Shouldn't we check out the crystal? We hadn't looked at it since we left Paris. Jenna had kept the metal box in her own bag. The way Jenna was shaking her head made me believe she also thought Miss Tregarthur could be faking. If so, we were heading for more trouble.

Demelza asked several times whether we should check to see if the light had reappeared inside the crystal. Each time Jenna said she wasn't going to open it because of the radiation. I could see that we didn't want either Demelza or Miss Tregarthur to know what had happened to the crystal. Keeping that a secret at least kept them guessing, rather than murdering us in our sleep. We might be needed if the crystal didn't work, everything would depend on that old man at the stones.

We arrived at the moorland town. After paying more money we did get a wheelchair. Not the sort of thing you'd expect. The chair was made out of basket material and had four large wheels. Still, it did what we wanted. We lifted Miss Tregarthur onto it and headed off to the inn. Disability access hadn't been invented and she had to be carried to a room upstairs.

All of this was taking money. If we didn't get out of here through the tunnel, there would be a lot more to worry about if we had to stay in this time – not least because it wouldn't be long before the First World War and I didn't like the idea of being put in the trenches to fight. Worrying wasn't going to stop us spending what we had and the inn gave us a large room.

There was space for Miss Tregarthur on a bed in an alcove. She wasn't talking, but she was taking sips of water – taking sips from Demelza. I watched closely to see if they were up to something. Probably I should have stayed awake all night.

-19-

LIES

In the morning Jenna went out to search for help with the rest of our journey – horse drawn help – we didn't want to have to wheel Miss Tregarthur all the way back to the moor. I'd offered to find someone but Jenna was firm that she wanted to make the arrangement. That probably meant she was planning something.

'I found a man with a cart and a horse. He'll come just after midday,' Jenna said. 'We should all fit it, fine so long as it doesn't rain. He's got some sacking we can put her on.' Jen pointed at the still unarousable figure of Miss Tregarthur. But just to check she gave the patient a poke which produced a groan and did I see a slight flicker of her eyes? Jenna gave me an eye rolling glance. 'And I've got a few provisions,' she said, showing me a lumpy sack.

'Don't forget the crystal,' Demelza said, pointing at the box we had brought from France. 'Do you think it will work again?'

'Probably doesn't matter,' Jenna said. 'If that white robed man turns up he can get the tunnel to work anyway. We probably don't need the crystal to actually work.'

I couldn't see why she sounded so confident. I wasn't sure anyone would turn up at the Hanging Stones to help us.

And another problem: 'Will your cart man get us across

the moor?' I asked. We could get up to the moorland village, to the inn we'd stayed at before, but after that there was no road or track.

'No,' Jenna replied and there was a lot in the look that she gave me which stopped me asking too many questions. 'We'll have to stay at the village inn and try to hire another horse in the morning. Then we can throw her over it for the last part of the journey.'

'Like we did with Zach and Demelza before,' I laughed. Demelza scowled.

There were parts to this plan I didn't understand. Why were we waiting for the cart? If we'd set off earlier we could probably have made the Hanging Stones without stopping. Why did we want to have another night at the inn? I had a feeling Jenna had set this up on purpose.

While we waited for the cart Jenna and I changed into the smocks we had worn before, smocks and boots. Ready for the moor. Demelza refused to change. The inn provided food. It seemed that potatoes were really common here along with pies and pasties. By the time the cart-man turned up I'd stuffed myself. Bad idea on a bumpy cart. There might be a road but it wasn't smooth. The roads would have to improve here if more cars appeared.

When the cart driver arrived he had a way of saying little but making us feel completely stupid. He made it clear that he expected me to sit up front with him, leaving the girls and Miss Tregarthur in the back along with our luggage. There might be sacking to sit on but the cart had obviously been carrying something smelly before us. I wondered if I would get away with the more comfortable ride. It was obvious that the man thought it was a male right to sit with him. Jenna and Demelza didn't fit into a high enough class to change that.

Jenna just pushed me to the front. 'Get up there, Mr Carter,' and she bowed with a grin. I was going to protest but Jen stopped me and anyway the pies in my stomach made this a good choice.

We rumbled off. Not the same route that we had walked before. We went through the town and followed a river for a while. The cart man kept stopping and talking to people he knew, lots of talk about food, food and manure. Our cart driver was the specialist manure deliverer, which explained the smell.

I turned to the others. Jenna sat looking backwards, watching the hedges disappear as the route took us up towards the moor. Miss Tregarthur on her sacking bed was nearer to the front. Demelza had stayed close to her and moved away quickly when I turned around. Did Jenna know what was going on? She almost seemed to be letting them get on with it, whatever 'it' might be.

The day had started overcast and as we went higher the misty drizzle started. I suppose that did dampen the smell but we were all quite soggy when we arrived at the village. We were used to this village inn, seen the changes over so many years in time. This time we had to take two rooms. There, apparently, wasn't one big enough to take us all.

'I'll go in with her,' Demelza said, pointing at Miss Tregarthur. 'Leave you two together.' She said 'together' in a pointed way. Losing Demelza for a night might be a great idea, but did we really want to leave those two alone?

'Fine,' said Jenna, before I had a chance to argue.

So, after another meal of potatoes and something I didn't recognise and probably didn't want to, we went to our rooms.

'See you in the morning,' Demelza winked at me as I closed our door. The rooms were next to each other.

'What the …?' I started as soon as we were alone.

'Shh.' Jenna went over to the wall between our rooms and listened.

Could we hear voices? If we could surely this had to be a bad idea. Nothing that Demelza and Miss Tregarthur did together was likely to be good.

Jenna wouldn't explain. 'I'll tell you in the morning,' she said, giving me a cuddle.

Down at breakfast – another potato meal – we were the only two guests.

'Shall I get Demelza?' I went towards the stairs.

'Worth a try, I suppose.' Jenna smiled.

I went upstairs, their door was open. The room was empty. I ran back down.

'Gone,' I shouted. 'We need to get after them, COME ON.'

Jenna didn't move and took another forkful of mash. 'Alvin, sit down and eat some more of this delicious meal. It might be your last.'

Why was Jenna so calm about this?

'But … but …,' I stammered.

'It's what I thought would happen,' Jenna said, with her mouth full. 'At least it's saved us from having to drag those two over the moor.'

'You think they've gone to the Hanging Stones?'

'Certainly,' Jenna said.

'Don't they need the crystal?' I looked around for the metal box.

'Demelza took it in the night,' Jenna laughed. 'You were out of it and snoring so you didn't hear her come in and take it.'

'You let her take it?' I could see Jenna had some plan and was really enjoying me being uncomfortable. I just had to hope this would work.

For a few more minutes we ate our breakfast and drank something we were told was tea. It definitely had a strange unpleasant taste. But we were both thirsty.

'You are right.' Jenna stood up. 'We do need to get after them.'

The envelope of money was empty, we had nothing to pay the inn. Demelza again. Without any money the landlady would find a way to make us work for payment. We wouldn't be able to get after them. We would have to run for it.

Jenna smiled again. 'They didn't take it all, I kept most of the notes.'

I felt stupid not to know what was happening. Jenna seemed to have worked all this out.

We paid and headed up the short hill to the moor.

We made for the top of the first tor, to give us a better view. Up on top the rain held off but the wind still blew hard, whisking tufts of grass in spirals. Clouds scuttled across the sky. The usual storm would come later. It was difficult to make out any movement. We sheltered from the wind and watched for a while.

'There.' I pointed.

In the distance we could see two figures. It was obvious that Miss Tregarthur might not be as sick as she had made out but she was still leaning heavily on Demelza. They were moving slowly, at that rate we could catch them before they reached the Hanging Stones. Demelza struggling in the clothes she had bought for Paris.

Jenna held back. 'Let them go, wait a bit.' Her words were blown away in the wind, while I just wondered what was going on.

I didn't argue and leant against the rocks. I didn't feel right. It had to have been that breakfast.

Further on, Jenna stopped again, suggesting we shared some of the stuff she'd bought in the town, carrying them in her lumpy sack. Not just potatoes, she had a couple of apples but neither of us felt like eating. My stomach still churned.

I was past asking questions. At least not knowing made me feel this might go better than I expected. We went on.

As we reached the bottom of Hanging Stone Hill we could see that Demelza was struggling badly. Miss Tregarthur could barely move on her own. They'd manage a few steps and then collapse with Demelza having to haul her to her feet. We weren't feeling great either. It wasn't just my stomach, I was feeling dizzy.

'I want them to get there first.' Jenna sat down holding her head. We were near a stream and could see what was happening further up the hill.

'Why?'

'This is my revenge.' Jenna's face reminded me of all the terrible things that had happened: the attack from the cavemen; the Black Death; the sentences to be burnt; the deportation across the world. Miss Tregarthur had brought all those upon us. All because we had stopped her from her promise to her father – a weird genetic experiment – for a group of captured teenagers.

I sat down beside Jenna and tried to throw stones into the stream. 'I still don't understand why she wanted us dead. It wasn't going to make anything better for her.' I threw another stone as hard as I could, it cracked against a bolder.

'Why did she want ... why did she need us to die?' I looked up. The noise of the stone must have reached the other two. Demelza turned and rushed to drag Miss Tregarthur up the hill.

'You.' Jenna held my hand to stop me throwing more stones. 'It was you she wanted dead. There must be another reason. We may be going to find out quite soon. Let's get after them.'

We climbed the hill, heading straight into the wind. That must have made it even harder for the other two. Black clouds were gathering. Even though it was only the middle of the day, the light was fading. We'd been through this sort of weather before, storms out here were common. But we were nearly there, nearly at the stones again. It wasn't just the other two who were struggling. My dizziness was worse, sounds started to feel a long way off, something was making us both unwell. Had we been affected by the radiation? We both had to sit again before making the final yards to the Hanging Stones.

Demelza stood at one side, appearing very pleased with herself. Miss Tregarthur sat a little further away with her back against another rock. In her hand the metal box with the crystal. The final push to reach the stones might have exhausted her but she gathered strength.

'Now you will die,' she howled. 'You will die out here with nothing. Can you feel the poison? She put it in your drink.'

Miss Tregarthur pointed to Demelza. That explained the awful tea we had drunk in the inn. The awful dizziness. Probably explained the missing money, you could buy anything, even the landlady.

'It won't be long now,' Miss Tregarthur gave her awful shriek of laughter. 'Soon you will be dead and then I will have you, soon you will be at my mercy, now we have the crystal.' She turned to Demelza. 'Give me the metal bar.'

Demelza handed it over. She must have found it in Paris and hidden it from us. Miss Tregarthur snarled and with one strike broke the tiny padlock.

'What?' she gasped as her hand came out of the box, not holding the crystal but one very large potato which fell from her hand and rolled on the grass. Seeing the empty box seemed to drain all her strength. She lay back panting and cursing.

'You don't have it,' Jenna cried, wincing as she held her stomach.

Were we both going to die from this poison? Jenna scrabbled in her sack and brought out another shape – the crystal. I didn't know how long it had been out of the lead box. Had the radiation restored the colours, brought it back to life? I couldn't be sure. I didn't think there was anything to see, but it was impossible to be certain.

Jenna had said she would bring the crystal back to the tunnel. Was it useless now, nothing that the tunnel would want? It would not help us now. I could feel myself slipping away. Had we been poisoned twice – by radiation and by Demelza? We were not going to make it home. It had all failed. At least you couldn't die twice.

Miss Tregarthur had started crawling towards us but Demelza got there first, wrenching the crystal from Jenna's hand. We hadn't the strength to stop her. She took the iron bar from Miss Tregarthur and returned to the Hanging Stones.

Demelza stood with the crystal in one hand and the iron bar in the other. Her hair blowing out behind her as the wind grew stronger, as wild and crazy as Miss Tregarthur had once looked.

'This is my time. I will defeat you all.' Demelza gave a shriek as she brought the bar down on the crystal.

Nothing, no noise from the tunnel.

Again and again she hit the stone.

The only sound was the storm coming.

Demelza smashed the crystal with all her strength, breaking it into fragments in her hand.

'Stop, stop,' cried Miss Tregarthur. 'I can feel it, it hurts me so,' she wept.

What did that mean? Had the crystal done something?

Demelza chucked the pieces of stone and the iron bar on the ground. 'No good, is it? Oh, and by the way it was her poison so I thought she should have some as well.' She pointed at Miss Tregarthur, who had crawled into a ball and was gently rocking. 'You are all going to die. I might as well go and find HG.'

Too weak to move, I looked at the face of Miss Tregarthur. She had crawled to the Hanging Stones and sat beside them. Perhaps her radiation sickness had been partly faked, but the poison had worked.

The sky was as dark as night. A fork of lightning flashed across the sky with the roar of thunder. Another lightning streak and another. My hair felt as though it stood on end, I could feel the electricity in the air. The battle in the sky raged on but brought no rain. All rain and wind stopped. Between the thunder crashes, the moor became silent. Waiting.

I saw Miss Tregarthur reach up to grasp the Hanging Stones but slide down in failure. She tried again. This time her whole body slipped under the strange rock shape, that looked like two balanced lumps of granite but in reality was this only one unmovable stone? She lay still and didn't move again. I heard one last choked gasp and after that there was nothing.

Miss Tregarthur had died.

The storm broke. The wind screamed into a gale again hurling itself across the moor, whipping up mud and stones in its path, hail burst out of the storm clouds. A massive bolt of lightning streaked through the sky, smashing down on to the Hanging Stones.

'The stones.' Jenna lifted a trembling hand and pointed.

The stones had been torn apart, at last becoming two and opening like a giant pincer. A pincer reaching down to take the fallen body of Miss Tregarthur, lifting her into the air. The mist of the time tunnel rose from the ground, so many colours until it faded to a black smoke.

New noises grew louder around us, the sound of great stones moving, sounds coming from deep down in the earth below. Miss Tregarthur's body rose up from the smoke before it seemed to melt into the rock. As her body disappeared a rumbling groan came from the ground. With a last dazzling flash of lightning the storm blew itself away. The Hanging Stones snapped back together. The three of us were left on the hill. Were we alone?

Jenna's face told me that Demelza's poison was doing its work. As I lay back, waiting for the end, the face of a man in his white robe stared down at me. Had he been here all the time?

In his hand a new crystal and the iron bar which he must have taken from Demelza. He lifted his hand and smacked down hard on his stone. That terrible tormented screech came again. The noise the tunnel had made before, when the crystal had been hit. The sound the tunnel made when part of it was hurt, when the stone from its heart was damaged. But this was not the same screech that we had heard before. This was a sound I knew. This was Miss Tregarthur's screech of pain.

I realised what awful thing had happened. Miss Tregarthur in death had been taken by the moor. Had she been taken to become the time tunnel?

I closed my eyes.

'Drink this.' The man held a flask to my mouth.

I drank, little point in refusing – I'd been poisoned anyway. Whatever it was he gave me made my head spin, made the whole world spin when I tried to open my eyes again. I don't remember a lot after that, some shouting, some horses and I think I heard Demelza saying it wasn't her fault.

-20-

The Family

I was on a bed and I hurt. It wasn't a feather bed with crisp white sheets, even though that might have been in my dreams. This was a hard wooden bed on a thin mattress and lumpy pillow in what had to be yet one more cave, lit only by faint green light. Not one I had been in before, but similar.

The light snapped me awake, green light and radiation. Where was I? I looked around. It was more like a normal room but still in a cave, with pieces of furniture, none of them new.

Jenna was sitting up on another bed and rubbing her eyes.

'Where, what … how,' I muttered. Jenna just shook her head.

Why weren't we dead? Stupid questions circled in my muddled mind.

The door opened. A cave with a door? And it was a massive wooden door with iron studs, the sort of thing that would keep people out or keep them in, a rusty creak as it opened.

A woman stepped in. Behind her I could see a corridor, not a cave but an ordinary house, ordinary except there were all sorts of paintings of people and ancient ornaments.

'Hello, Alvin,' she said. 'It's been so long.' She stood looking at me.

I stared back – cave, door, and another person knowing my name. I tried to stand, the dizziness returned.

She came towards me. 'Steady.' She placed her hand on my shoulder and her touch didn't feel so strange. I guess she was about as old as my mother – as old as my mother would have been if she hadn't been killed by Neanderthals. She had a sort of old hippy appearance, wearing a long patterned green dress, strings of wooden beads around her neck, and her fair hair in ringlets. Why did she seem familiar, what she'd said made it sound as though we'd met before?

'Who are you?' Jenna stood up from her bed, staggered and sat down again.

'Anna, I'm Anna and …' She turned to the door. 'This is Peter. And he's brought you food and drink.'

Peter entered with a tray. He must have been a bit older than me. Dressed in the sort of working smock we'd seen before, we'd worn before.

'Hi.' Peter smiled and set the tray down on a wooden box in our cave, before leaving.

'What's …' I started.

'Wait.' Anna held up the palm of her hand to stop me. 'Eat and rest and after that we can talk.'

I could see Jenna wasn't happy with this plan, but we were both too weak to argue.

'I will return in a little while,' Anna said in her soft voice as she made for the door. 'There are more clothes,' she pointed to a wooden cupboard standing at one side of the cave. Then she was gone. Did I hear a lock turn in the door?

There was a large jug of some juice, a reddish yellow colour. It tasted sweet and we drank it all. Whatever happened had left us parched. Rolls of bread, butter and cheese made up the food.

'This still isn't food from our own time.' Jenna ate as she sat on her bed. 'This cave is a bit like …' She paused. 'It's a bit like somewhere we've been before.'

I understood Jenna's confusion. This cave, what had happened at the Hanging Stones, Anna and Peter ... everything felt slightly blurred.

'That green light,' I pointed to the cave roof. 'Something to do with radiation. Is it dangerous?' I ate another roll.

'Did Anna lock the door?' Jenna looked around. 'There could be another way out, down there.' She pointed into the darkness of the cave where I could just make out the start of a passage.

'Do we run for it?' I said, even though I knew we weren't up to running anywhere.

Jenna shook her head. 'Have to see what happens here. We have to find out what's been going on.'

Finishing the food and drink we felt a little stronger and checked out the clothes in the wooden cupboard. There were all sorts of things, not just clothes: a shovel, a rucksack like the ones we had taken on our first walk with Miss Tregarthur, a length of rope, a box of old instruments, clothes which weren't really better than what we had been wearing and an ancient hunting knife.

'Do I keep this with me?' I weighed the knife in my hand.

'No, but maybe keep it somewhere close in case we need it,' Jenna said.

I put the knife under the lumpy pillow. The effort of searching had exhausted us and both of us lay back on the beds. I think we must have slept. We were woken again by Anna.

'Time to meet the others.' Anna stood by the open door. 'Come.'

‘What happened to Demelza?’ Jenna stopped at the door.

‘She’s fine,’ Anna replied.

‘I don’t want to know she’s fine,’ Jenna cut across Anna’s singsong voice. ‘I want to know she’s locked up and not poisoning people.’

Anna turned. ‘You don’t need to worry about her, she can’t get out. Come with me and all will be explained.’

I really doubted about the ‘all’ that would be explained. If this was anything to do with Miss Tregarthur I felt sure that ‘all’ would leave some things out, usually the important things.

Anna held the door open. The hallway stretched out in front of us, dark, wood panelled, a worn carpet and all of this looked old.

We followed Anna down the hall hung with paintings on each side – pictures of old ancient people in red robes lined with fur, pictures of animals hunting, below the pictures were huge dusty jars and pots. A suit of armour stood in an alcove. Further down the hall a row of pegs hung with coats … I stopped and stared. Coats of all types – fur, wool, tweed, and jackets with modern names I recognised. A mixture of clothes across time.

Anna gave a quiet laugh and led us on. Another door.

We entered. Light from two tall windows flooded the room. Through these windows a wild landscape stretched out in front of us. Black rocks of a tor visible in the distance. A bleak vision and it meant we were still somewhere on the moor. Looking out across the brown countryside I could see dots of purple heather. Heather? I knew that name from someone, didn’t I? Someone had told me it was heather. I shook my head, my mind still felt blurred as it had done since we woke up. Was that the poison?

The white robed man had given me something, how had he known what to do? Maybe Miss Tregarthur had poisoned other people before. Maybe they all used the same poison.

It was raining. A loud cough made me turn from the window.

In the middle of the room stood a long polished wooden table. There were ten or eleven chairs. Each one was occupied. Each person so different. A picture of different times; Anna with her hippy look, a woman in an army khaki uniform, another woman dressed as a nurse, another man in a suit, all were at ease even though none of them seemed to match. None of them matched the same period of time.

At the head of the table sat the man in his white robe, smiling. 'Welcome back, Alvin. Welcome too, Jenna. Sit. My name, if you don't remember, is Baylock, Baylock Tregarthur.'

Was this the same robed man? Surely not the ancient man who had saved us during the earthquake. If not him, it could be the same man who'd given me something for the poison. Whoever he was, he still he had the look of a Tregarthur.

It was a good job there were vacant seats because I was ready to pass out. I felt hands guide me down to sit. Jenna and I flicked glances at each other and at the door.

'Run,' I tried to say but I had no strength to stand, we were at their mercy. Even if we got away we had no idea where we were or when in time we had arrived at this house. But another Tregarthur, that meant real danger.

'Stay calm, there is no danger for you here,' Baylock said, his voice just ramped up my fear.

'Calm,' said Anna, as she laid her hand on my arm.

'I wanted you to meet the others,' Baylock waved his arm at the people around the table. 'They have to return to their work, the good that they do, but you will meet them again, I'm sure. You have met some of them before. They are all family, of sorts.'

There were nods around the table. I wasn't sure but they felt familiar, almost as though I was part of this family, how could that be true? Were all of them Tregarthurs? Did it mean I was a Tregarthur? Had Jenna been right? Was Miss Tregarthur really my aunt? I didn't resemble any of them, did I?

'Some stay here and some leave forever,' Baylock slowed each word, a haunting speech. 'Not all those passing through do so for the good. Masterson, Brigitte – you met her in France – we know them all. They are our failures. They leave but they will never escape. We can find them – Alice knew where to find them.'

His words filled me with their awful truth. This was a terrible network. A mafia of dangerous time travelling individuals. No wonder Miss Tregarthur had found Masterson – he was part of this. They all were.

'What about Miss Tregarthur?' Jenna said. 'Another one of those failures?'

'All in good time,' Baylock said, and it was going to be as I had expected, we would never be told everything.

The chairs pushed back and the others left, only Baylock and Anna remained.

'Come closer.' Anna pointed to empty chairs nearer to their end of the table. We hesitated. Did we want to move closer to them?

Baylock laughed, 'It is alright, you are safe here.'

I didn't feel safe but we still moved nearer to him.

'Your mother brought you here,' Baylock said, and looked at me for a response.

My vacant expression must have explained a lot.

'She never told you?' Anna said, as though she didn't believe that could have happened.

I shook my head. Baylock shot a glance at Anna before turning back at me. 'Then there is so much for you to learn.'

'Wait a minute,' Jenna butted in. 'This is all weird and wonderful and feels like some family gathering, but I'm not sure I believe we are safe. For a start where is Demelza? And what happened to Miss Tregarthur?'

'So many questions,' Baylock sighed.

We were not going to get all the answers at all, just bits they wanted us to hear.

'We are the guardians …,' Baylock said, in a deep loud serious voice.

'Not doing a very good job of it,' Jenna interrupted before whispering to me. 'Sounds like a silly old fart to me.'

I nodded. Baylock's face twisted and his eyes flared. I don't expect he was used to being challenged. Or being called an old fart. But he quickly changed back to the bland smile he'd had before. The face he'd hidden had looked even more like that of Miss Tregarthur.

'Alice was a problem, she always has been difficult and she always will be.' Baylock gave another of his sighs. He was trying to show us the weight of all the problems he had to sort out. Another alarm went off in my head at the 'always will be'. I thought she was dead but we were dealing with time travel. Dead might not be really dead.

That made me think about my mum, she must have left out many things in my life – like this place and these people. Maybe I couldn't trust her even if we could go back in time and save her.

'Why do you say my mother brought me here?' I said.

'She did and more than that.' Anna would have gone on. Baylock motioned her to stop and took over.

'As I said we are the guardians of the moor and the travel in time.' Baylock checked that Jenna wasn't going to interrupt.

But it was me that butted in, 'You said you couldn't control the time tunnel?'

'Tunnel? Ah yes, I see what you mean, but it isn't always a tunnel.' Baylock was talking down to me. I didn't like it.

'Then what is it?' I snapped.

'Each new circle of travel starts in a different way, starting inside the rock, fighting to find its way out. That was the tunnel you found, one that took so many years to find the way. She had to fight so hard. She fought until the end.'

'You say 'she', but the last sound I heard on the moor was Miss Tregarthur's screech.'

'One cycle leaves when there is another to take their place. Alice became that person with her death. When Alice died she was taken into the moor, she has become the voice of the moor, she has become the way to travel time. If you like, Alice Tregarthur has become the new time tunnel.' Baylock stopped.

I felt a cold shiver as his words sank into my head. The Miss Tregarthur we had seen disappearing into the ground, she had become the time tunnel. She wasn't dead at all. That was the end for us, she would never take us to any place or any time.

'What happened to the old tunnel, whoever SHE was?' My voice shook as I spoke.

'You felt her true and final death,' Anna broke in. 'That last storm was the end for her.'

I had so many questions but there was no time to ask. With a crash and the splintering of glass, a rock smashed through the window and skidded across the long table. Another followed.

Baylock's words, the shattering noise, I wanted to run but felt frozen to my chair. Through the window was a sight I had never wanted to see again. Outside a band of men ready to throw more stones, ready to attack. Men in furs holding great clubs. The cavemen were here.

'GO, RUN,' Baylock shouted to Anna. 'Get the others.' Then, to us: 'You must get to the cave room. This is our fight, ours alone. We will fight them. RUN.' More rocks crashed through the broken window.

'GO, GO!' His words finally broke through. I had to move.

The cavemen screamed and charged.

'The key' Baylock called out.

Anna threw a key to us as she left.

'Lock yourselves in, fix the bar and wait for us. Do not leave. Wait for us. But go NOW.' Baylock dodged a flying rock.

We tried to run but only staggered along the hall with shouts coming from behind us, Baylock was gathering the others to him. We pushed through the heavy door into the cave room.

'Bar,' cried Jenna.

A heavy iron bar stood at one side. Picking it up I slid it across the door, it was held in place by two iron hoops. This door was made to protect.

As we slid the bar into place and turned the lock we could hear the noise of fighting in the hallway. Baylock had been right to get us out of the way. Even if we had been saved from a poison death, it had taken our strength and we collapsed on to the beds.

'How did cavemen get here?' I groaned. 'I thought they couldn't travel in the tunnel.' Last time when we had been chased by cavemen they had stopped at the entrance to the tunnel, unable to go further, and that had happened to anyone from their own time trying to follow us.

'Can it be true? What Baylock said happened to Miss Tregarthur?' As Jenna said that we heard hammering on the other side of the door.

'Help, help, let me in,' came Demelza's frantic shouts.

'Do we?' I looked at Jenna.

Jenna shrugged and went to move the iron bar and open the door.

'Quick.' Demelza pushed through. 'They're coming.' She looked over her shoulder and we could see a group of the cavemen running towards us, more rocks in their hands.

We slammed the door, locked it and slid the iron bar across. Rocks thudded into the wood outside and I could hear the cavemen crashing their clubs to break down the door. For the moment it held. Would it stand this sort of attack? Had it been made for this?

We had to hope that the cavemen would give up and take the fight to the others in the house – unless everyone was dead already.

Jenna stood at the cupboard and threw me the length of rope. 'Tie her up. We don't want a battle with her as well as that lot outside. She's probably still got a load of poison ready to use.'

Demelza squealed but I still roped her arms and tied her to the metal hoops on the door. 'If they break in they can have her first,' I said, and turned away from her squeals.

Shouldn't we have left her to die? Demelza was dangerous. But perhaps we did need to keep her and to get her home if the time tunnel would ever work again.

It had been so long ago that my mother had said this would never stop unless we took everyone home. She said that just before she died. We had left several dead people across time. Did we have to get them home as well? Did leaving Demelza to die make any difference? We'd done it now, let her in with us. I supposed there was a chance we could use her as a diversion for the cavemen if we had to. Except Jenna would never let that happen.

-21-

A Battle in Time.

It wasn't long before Demelza tried her usual tricks. 'Don't you want to know what's going on?' she said.

'Of course we do, but I doubt you know anything,' I said, and waited for more.

'I overheard them talking.' Demelza was trying to sound convincing.

'So we untie you and you tell us everything?' Jenna gave a sarcastic laugh.

'Of course.' Demelza didn't seem to get the sarcasm.

'How about you tell us what you know or we untie you and push you back outside.' Jenna looked away.

'You wouldn't, would you?' Demelza returned to squealing as another rock thudded against the door.

'Actually, why don't we push her back outside anyway,' I said, standing up from my bed. 'At least that would stop her going on.'

'Good idea.' Jenna nodded.

'NO, NO, please.' Demelza slid down to the ground on her knees, her hands still held by the rope. She obviously believed that we would carry out the threat because that was what she would have done.

'Then start talking.' Jenna made it sound as though that was her only option.

'Ok, ok.' Demelza waited for me to sit back on my bed. 'The time tunnel isn't a tunnel at all, it's alive.'

'We know that already, I've heard enough from you,' I said, as the crashing at the door grew even louder.

Demelza tried to pull away and stuttered, 'B-b-but you don't know what's happened.'

'Go on,' Jenna prompted.

'Miss Tregarthur has become the tunnel. It's what happens when they die. But it doesn't last forever. That's why Miss Tregarthur wanted …' She stopped.

'Wanted what?' I realised that she had said more than she intended.

'Nothing,' Demelza said, but she knew it was too late.

'The door Alvin,' Jenna pointed and I started to get up again.

'NO.' Demelza held up her tied hands.

I walked towards her.

'She wanted you dead,' she muttered.

'Why?' Jenna sounded puzzled.

'Alvin is one of them,' Demelza replied to Jenna: 'It's something to do with this cave, this house, the moor. His mother,' she nodded at me, 'she came here when she was pregnant.' Demelza turned to me. 'Alvin, you were born here. You are part of it all.'

I was too bewildered to ask anything. All sorts of thoughts buzzed in my brain, from the beginning there had been a connection between my mum and the Tregarthurs.

Demelza went on: 'It seems that if you're born here, with that green light thing,' she pointed to the roof of the cave, 'It makes you one of them, the moor will get you in the end, when you die.'

'Doesn't explain why Miss Tregarthur wanted Alvin dead,' Jenna said.

Demelza went on: 'If Alvin died before her then he would have been next. You heard that awful sound when she hit the crystal, well it's like that a lot of the time for the tunnel. If Alvin died before her, she wouldn't have had to do it, she was expecting to carry on moving through time and getting away with it.'

'And you learnt all this from overhearing their conversation?' I didn't believe her. I didn't want to hear. Did Miss Tregarthur mean me to be the one screaming whenever she hit the crystal, wanting to be taken through time?

Jenna jumped up. 'Miss Tregarthur told you all about it. You knew all about this each time you and Zach tried to kill us. Now tell us the rest.'

'That's about it.' Demelza tried to shy away.

'No it's not,' Jenna shouted and moved closer. 'Why Alvin? Why didn't she just kill one of the others here?'

'I told you, you have to be born here. Most of them weren't.' Demelza was pushing herself back against the door, more scared of Jenna than the cavemen.

'Why didn't she just do it herself, just kill me. There were lots of times she could have done that?' I asked but I thought I knew the answer.

'Well … she … she couldn't,' Demelza stammered again.

Jenna clenched her fists as she shouted, 'That's why you had to kill him, isn't it? She needed someone else to kill him? Couldn't have the blood on her own hands or it wouldn't work.

If she killed Alvin herself, it wouldn't save her.'

Demelza gave a miserable nod.

'Me or her?' I asked and she nodded again. 'I still don't see why it had to be me? What made her go after me in the first place? There must be someone here who she could have used instead. What about Baylock?'

'Don't know about him, she never talked about him,' Demelza said.

'But why me?'

'She had trouble with your mum,' Demelza added. 'Trouble with her brother, you, your dad, all of you. I don't know exactly why she hated all of you.'

Was that the only reason? I could understand how we might not have been one happy family but was that enough reason to pursue me over thousands of years?

Demelza seemed to give up keeping things from us. 'Alvin, you were the youngest. The younger a person is the more powerful the tunnel becomes. If she could get you killed, she believed she could go back to the time of the cavemen and complete her promise.'

'Instead she brought the cavemen here,' I said, and listened, but the fighting had quietened down outside, we still heard shouts in the distance. 'How has she brought them here?'

'I don't know,' Demelza said, and that sounded as though it might actually be true.

'Who was the person in the last tunnel? The one we've been using,' Jenna said, in a cold quiet voice. 'Baylock seemed to know her.'

Demelza hung her head before telling us. 'It was Miss Tregarthur's sister. Her baby sister. Her mother was much

much younger than her dad and she died giving birth. The baby, her sister, lived for only a little while. But she had been born here so was next in line.'

The awfulness of that piece of news took time to hit my brain. Miss Tregarthur used her dead sister to travel time, to bring down that awful pain on her when she struck the crystal. 'How could she do that?'

'She felt her sister had killed her mother when she was born,' Demelza said.

I didn't want to hear anymore and I didn't have a chance. There was a massive shout, the sound of stamping feet running towards us and the door almost exploded with splintering wood. It held, but a gap opened and we could see straight through into the wrecked hallway. A group of cavemen, carrying a huge tree trunk, had battered the door. We could see their snarling faces. One put his hand through the hole and started pulling at the wood.

Demelza turned and sunk her teeth into the caveman's arm before shouting at me, 'UNTIE ME, LET ME GO,' and pulling at the rope holding her to the door, while she screamed. The men were preparing to charge again with their battering ram.

Without thinking, I grabbed the knife from under my pillow and slashed through Demelza's ropes just as they hit the door again. The metal bar rattled and bent. Would the door stand another charge? The hunting knife wouldn't be a lot of use if we had to fight them all.

'We run,' cried Jenna pointing to the darkness at the end of the cave. And we did. Behind us, another crash as the cavemen tried again to break through. It wouldn't be long before they were after us.

The only escape was through the passage we had seen at the end of our cave. We had no idea where it went. It was just wide enough for us to pass along one at a time, a dim green light radiated from the stone. Not long before we came to a fork.

'Which way?' I panted.

'Upwards,' Demelza pointed to the left hand fork.

The grunting screams were behind us – the cavemen had broken through the door. On we ran. They were closing on us. The passage opened up into a wider lighter space.

I stopped, still holding the knife. I might have a chance to hold them up for a while in the narrow space behind me but not in this wider passage. There were too many. I wouldn't hold them for long and had to hope it would be enough time for the others to get away.

Jenna just grabbed my arm and dragged me on, no argument, at least we could run faster in the wider space. We were still weak from the poison. The way grew steeper, taking us higher, taking all our strength. Ahead the light was stronger. We could see the end of the passage, something whizzed through the air.

Demelza yelled and tumbled to the floor as a rock hit her. I dragged her to her feet. On we ran, more rocks fizzed behind us. We reached daylight and tumbled out through bushes. We were back on the moor. Not far in front of us stood the Hanging Stones. Baylock stood near them. He was alone. Not far behind came the screaming, howling cavemen.

Baylock's robe blew out in the wind, the wild Tregarthur look on his face. 'Onwards,' he pointed to the stones and we ran forward.

He turned with an ancient rifle in his hands. As the cavemen appeared from the passage he pulled the trigger. With an enormous roar and flash one of the cavemen fell to the ground. The others fled back into the passage with grunts and screams.

'Won't stop them for long.' Baylock reloaded and called to me. 'Alice has had her vengeance. I would not let her travel in time to make money and destroy the world, neither her nor her father with his dangerous ideas.'

I could see that Baylock had been injured, blood oozing from a wound on his leg and from one on his chest.

'Alice has broken time, opened the way for this attack, brought back the people from the time she has travelled. All the bad and evil will soon be upon us.'

If he meant all the evil, then cavemen could be the least of the problems, what about all those villagers with the Black Death?

'You must take your chance.' He handed me a sack. Inside a new crystal and the iron bar Miss Tregarthur had used to call the time tunnel.

'Go now,' he said, raising the gun as the cavemen started to come forward again. 'Nothing will be the same, my family is destroyed, there will be no guardians any more. You must find your own path.'

Should we stay and help or head for home?

'Come on,' shouted Demelza.

We had tried. Helped when everything seemed so bad. It was time to leave. We went to the stones. I called to the tunnel. I called to Miss Tregarthur since Baylock said she had the power of time travel. From the stones came her wild tormenting laugh.

'Hit the crystal,' Demelza tried to wrestle the iron bar from me. 'Hit the crystal.'

Jenna pushed Demelza to the ground, took the bar and smashed it down onto the shimmering stone.

We had heard the awful wail before but this time it was far worse. It came from the voice we knew, Miss Tregarthur's voice. Jenna struck again and again. Behind us the cavemen retreated, this time it was the sound that made them slink away with their hands over their ears.

I could see where they hid. Baylock was right, nothing would stop them in the end. Was this attack planned in their minds thousands of years before?

The colours of the time travel mist appeared below the Hanging Stones. I had no faith in Miss Tregarthur taking us to our own time and to our homes. I told Jenna to keep threatening to hit the crystal. It was what Miss Tregarthur deserved.

Strangely her voice echoed out across the moor.

'I will send you to your own time, to your own homes, that is what you deserve.'

What did she mean? Deserve? We stepped forward into the mist, the blue colour appearing – the colour which told us we were going home. I held Jenna's hand. Demelza was in front and running. The mist swirled around us, sucking us in, moving the world and time around us. We came down hard, hitting the stones. Miss Tregarthur made sure we had a painful journey.

We were through. Back on to the moor. But in the distance I could hear the noises of cars and planes. Noises we would never have heard in earlier times.

'We're back,' Jenna sobbed.

'Back?' I said, remembering I would have so many more problems at home.

'Duck,' shouted Demelza as a fighter jet screamed towards us, blasting the moor with exploding bullets.

Yes, we were back, but Miss Tregarthur had changed time.

- END OF BOOK 4 -

CillianPress
www.cillianpress.co.uk

ABOUT THE AUTHOR

This is Alex Mellanby's fourth novel in the Tregarthur Series. His writing has finally driven him over the edge of sense and he now exists in a shadowy realm of fiction. Whether he can save Alvin and Jenna remains uncertain and the future is much worse than the past.

www.tregarthurseries.com

Join in on the conversation at
facebook.com/tregarthurseries

www.ingramcontent.com/pod-product-compliance
Ingram Content Group UK Ltd.
Pitfield, Milton Keynes, MK11 3LW, UK
UKHW041845200726
13854UKWH00005BA/2147

9 781909 776203